"I find myself at a loss.

I know you're up to someth
since my family has taken y
hardly toss you out on your

"I live here now," Emma sai
disagree.

"And why is that?"

"You didn't want any explanations," she reminded him.

"Perhaps I was too hasty."

"The information window is closed." Her ironic smile
made his temper spark, but he was determined to keep
the upper hand.

"What if we agree to an exchange? One piece of info
for another."

"I don't need to know anything about you. I don't care."

"Look at me." He strode to where she sat, pulled her to
her feet. "Actually, there's only one thing I really need to
know."

"What's that?"

"I'll show you," he said, capturing her mouth beneath
his.

* * *

Christmas in the Billionaire's Bed
is part of The Kavanaghs of Silver Glen series:
In the mountains of North Carolina, one family
discovers that wealth means nothing without love.

* * *

If you're on Twitter,
tell us what you think of Harlequin Desire!
#harlequindesire

Dear Reader,

It's always fun for me when I have the opportunity to do a Christmas book. December is a moment in the year that reminds me of many happy times from my own childhood and from the days when I had wide-eyed toddlers.

The holiday season is filled with hope and healing. For Emma and Aidan, it's a chance to repair a broken relationship from long ago. They have little in common on the surface. And their love seems doomed from the start. But in the elegant town of Silver Glen, with snowflakes swirling in the air and fires burning in every hearth, they find some Christmas magic.

All my best to you and yours during this season of love and hope. Count your blessings, and may all your dreams come true...

Fondly,

Janice Maynard

CHRISTMAS IN THE BILLIONAIRE'S BED

—

JANICE MAYNARD

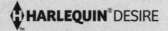

Recycling programs
for this product may
not exist in your area.

ISBN-13: 978-0-373-73357-6

Christmas in the Billionaire's Bed

Printed in U.S.A.

™ www.Harlequin.com

Books by Janice Maynard

Harlequin Desire

Silhouette Desire

*The Men of Wolff Mountain
◊The Kavanaghs of Silver Glen

Other titles by this author available in ebook format.

JANICE MAYNARD

is a *USA TODAY* bestselling author who lives in beautiful east Tennessee with her husband. She holds a BA from Emory and Henry College and an MA from East Tennessee State University. In 2002 Janice left a fifteen-year career as an elementary school teacher to pursue writing full-time. Now her first love is creating sexy, character-driven, contemporary romance stories.

Janice loves to travel and enjoys using those experiences as settings for books. Hearing from readers is one of the best perks of the job! Visit her website, www.janicemaynard.com, and follow her on Facebook and Twitter.

For all the wonderful authors who paved the way at Mills & Boon. I read your stories growing up, took trips around the world, and dreamed of writing my own romantic heroes one day...

One

Aidan Kavanagh stared at the cream vellum card edged with tiny holly leaves and berries and shook his head in reluctant admiration.

Game. Set. Match.

His mother had won the war without firing a single shot. The last thing Aidan wanted to do was visit Silver Glen, North Carolina, during the holidays, but Maeve knew he wouldn't miss his own brother's wedding.

The first of his siblings, Liam, had tied the knot recently as well. That event had been a huge, splashy society affair at Zoe's home in Connecticut—a hop, skip and a jump from New York City. This time Aidan wouldn't be so lucky.

It wasn't that he didn't love Silver Glen. He did. But

going home for Christmas brought back too many ugly memories. So, he chose to visit his large, close-knit family at other times of the year: Easter, Mother's Day, the Fourth of July…and October, when the fall foliage in the mountains was at its peak.

But December? No. In the last decade, he had managed it only once and only then because one of his brothers had been in the hospital. Aidan would have felt like a total jerk if he had let his family down.

That visit had been both uncomfortable and unpleasant. His mother and brothers had walked on eggshells around him, everyone far too aware that Aidan carried the weight of past tragedy. He'd done his damnedest to prove to them he was fine…that he had moved on.

Unfortunately, no one had been convinced by his deliberate facade of Christmas cheer. Least of all Aidan himself. Because the truth was, December sucked. He was fine. His life was good. He was content. But not even his family knew the worst of what had happened so long ago.

He stood and stretched, tossing the offending invitation on his desk. The view from his office window stretched from the Statue of Liberty all the way to the George Washington Bridge. Aidan loved New York City. The constant pulse of life. The fact that he could stop for lox and bagels at three in the morning and no one batted an eye.

Most of all, he loved the anonymity. No one here cared about his past or even his future. The emotional breathing room had become as essential to him as food or water.

Growing up in Silver Glen provided an idyllic childhood—at least until his father's death when Aidan was a young teen. The little alpine-like town would always be home. But living in a fishbowl where everyone knew his business became unbearable when he was twenty-one and his entire world crumbled around him.

Moving to New York had been his salvation. With a hefty nest egg of Kavanagh money—long since repaid—he'd started a high-end real estate company. The lessons he'd learned as a youth working in his family's swank hotel stood him in good stead. Although the Kavanaghs were very wealthy, the crème de la crème here in the city took that definition to a far greater level. Aidan enjoyed the challenge of matching socialites and business magnates with their perfect homes on the rooftops of Manhattan.

His phone pinged, reminding him of an upcoming appointment. Once more he sat down, then picked up his favorite pen and rolled the heavy gold cylinder between his fingers. He had inked his first real estate deal with this pen. Beyond the leather blotter, the wedding invitation lay innocently. He read it a second time, finding its elegant cursive font no less stomach tightening than he had before.

December 20th. That meant Aidan would need to be in Silver Glen no later than the weekend before. Knowing his mother, she would undoubtedly have planned a series of social events to fill the days leading up to the wedding. And then he would be expected to hang around until the family celebrated Christmas together on the 25th. Almost two weeks. Might as well be a lifetime.

He glanced at the paper calendar his assistant kept updated on the corner of his desk. She was as tech savvy as the next person, but she had discovered that Aidan liked to keep tabs on his schedule in more than one medium. The month of December was notably blank.

No one, with very few exceptions, shopped for high-dollar real estate during December. His clients were too busy hosting parties, overspending on their spoiled children and taking trips to exotic locations. Which meant, unfortunately, that Aidan was free to do as he pleased.

Or in this instance as he did *not* please.

For a moment, he flashed back, his vision blinded to the present but very aware of the past. Two young women. Both beautiful. Both charming. Both full of life and fun. And he had lost each of them.

The familiar burning sensation in his gut was more than a mix of guilt and regret. It was a longing for what he would never have. Absolution. A woman and a family to call his own.

Spending Christmas at Silver Glen would undoubtedly resurrect a host of old memories that he'd rather not face. But if he were honest, the memories lived with him everywhere. The painful part of going home was having other people *share* the memories. The empathy and concern on the faces of his siblings and his mother would be his downfall.

He didn't want their love to heal him. He didn't deserve that. And he didn't want to *feel* anything. Family knew his weak spots. Family refused to let him cling to the cloak of indifference that made it possible to live from day to day.

Aidan Kavanagh was a charming shell of a man, interested only in closing a deal or cashing a check. Ask anyone. The persona was one he had crafted carefully to keep people away. After loving and losing three times in his life, he was through with emotion…with caring.

In Silver Glen, especially at the holidays, he would have to be himself—the young man who had enjoyed life and reached for happiness with the careless naïveté of the innocent. He would be forced to open himself up to the warmth of family celebrations that would make him terribly vulnerable.

Could he do that and still survive?

Doggedly, he reached for the peace he had created here in the city. Emotional anonymity. A pleasant shield that kept other people from inflicting hurt.

He didn't hurt. He *wouldn't* hurt. Loving his family was a given. But beyond that, he had nothing to offer. Loving and losing meant vicious, unrelenting pain. Only a fool would walk that path again.

Emma Braithwaite leaned into the bay window, perched precariously on a stepladder that had seen better days. Creating the shop's storefront display was usually the highlight of her workweek. Today's theme, not exactly original, was teapots. Twitching the edge of a lace drape into place, she tried to visualize what her handiwork looked like from the street.

On the other side of the glass, a woman stopped and waved madly. Emma smiled. Even through the reverse gold lettering that spelled out Silver Memories, she recognized her visitor. Maeve Kavanagh, matriarch of the Kavanagh family—mother to seven sexy, über-masculine, wildly attractive grown men, and heir to the Kavanagh fortune.

Maeve's husband's ancestors had literally created the town after discovering a rich vein of silver deep in the mountain. The family story took a tragic turn when Maeve's feckless husband, Reggie, became obsessed with finding the remnants of the mine. One day he climbed into the hills and never returned.

But that bit of local color was from long ago. Maeve was now a vibrant woman in her early sixties who managed to keep tabs on her brood and run a thriving business up at the Silver Beeches Lodge. A little bell tinkled over the door as Maeve entered. Her dark auburn hair—with only slight traces of silver—was done up in a stylish bun.

Emma climbed down from the ladder and straightened her skirt.

Maeve waved an envelope at her. "I know etiquette dictates I mail this to you, but I couldn't wait. Here. Take it."

Emma accepted the cream-colored envelope with a grin. The missive was thick, the paper expensive. When she opened it and examined the contents, she understood the older woman's enthusiasm. "Another wedding?"

Maeve's smug smile said everything. "Indeed. And this time right here in Silver Glen. I know it seems hurried, but Dylan's adoption of Cora will be final on the day after Christmas. He and Mia want to be married and have their family complete."

Emma tucked everything back in the envelope. "I'm honored to be invited."

Emma and Mia had met several months ago at a coffee shop around the corner from Silver Memories. Since then they had become friends. Emma knew Maeve had been extremely kind in including Mia's parents as hosts for the wedding. The Larins had given birth to Mia late in life and now lived in Florida on a fixed income.

Maeve waved a hand. "Don't be silly. You're practically part of my family now. Mia raves about you, and I've enjoyed getting to know you these last few months."

Not long after Emma opened her store, Maeve had dropped by to shop for a set of occasional tables to use in a lounge at the Silver Beeches. It was thanks to Maeve that word had spread and the small shop had become a success so quickly.

"May I ask you something personal, Maeve?"

"Of course."

"Is the baby's father in the picture? Mia never speaks of him, and I didn't want to upset her by asking."

Maeve shook her head. "Dear Mia chose to have a baby via a sperm donor. When she and Dylan got together, he fell in love with little Cora. They make a beautiful family, don't you think?"

Emma smiled wistfully. "They certainly do." She had often seen Dylan and Mia and the baby out walking on afternoons when the weather was still warm.

Silver Glen was a small, cozy town, even though it boasted a strong tourist economy. Movie stars shooting on location often took up residence, as well as wealthy travelers who loved the peace of the mountains. The town's alpine flavor reminded Emma of a Swiss village.

"There's one more thing," Maeve said, her expression cajoling. "Mia told me you're not going home to England for Christmas, is that right?"

"Yes. I spent two weeks in September with my mother for her birthday. She's handling the loss of my father better than I expected. And she has plans to tour the Greek Isles during the latter part of December with a group of her friends."

"Then I want you to spend the holidays with us. Mia's parents are coming only for the wedding itself. So I know Mia would enjoy having you around. We're gathering for several occasions at Dylan and Mia's home. My older son and his wife are still building their new house. And of course, we'll have some special events up at the lodge, too. What do you think?"

Emma didn't know what to say. She wasn't afraid to be alone. In fact, her childhood had been solitary more times than not. She enjoyed the peace and tranquility of her own thoughts. And she was not a Kavanagh. Surely her presence would be awkward.

Maeve spotted a silver rattle and a matching small cup from the 1950s. "I knew I remembered seeing these," she said triumphantly. "One of my college sorority sisters just became a grandma for the first time. This will be the perfect gift."

As Emma rang up the purchase and took Maeve's credit card, she wondered how large a wedding the Kavanaghs were planning. And then another thought struck. One that made her heart race.

"Will all of your family be able to attend on such short notice?" Emma had never actually confessed to Maeve that she knew one of her sons very well.

For the first time, Maeve lost a bit of her excitement. "I hope so. My third son, Aidan, lives in New York. We don't see him all that often. And besides…"

She trailed off, her expression indicating that she had traveled somewhere unpleasant in her mind.

Emma wanted to know badly. "Besides what?"

Maeve's lips twisted, her eyes shadowed. "Aidan had a very bad experience some years ago. It happened at Christmas. He comes home to visit, but not at the holidays."

"And this wedding?"

"We hope he'll make the effort, but who knows…"

What would Aidan think if he saw Emma ensconced in the bosom of his family? She hadn't set eyes on him in a decade. Her original intent in coming to Silver Glen during the late summer had been to speak with him and bring some closure to what had been a painful time in their lives. She had hurt him badly, and she wanted to explain and make amends. But she discovered he no longer lived in the town of his birth.

Her recent birthday had brought home the fact that life passed quickly. Regret was an emotion fraught with negativity. After healing a decade-long rift with her father back in the spring, she had realized she wanted to move forward and to make better decisions than she had in her early twenties.

It was entirely possible that Aidan had not clung to the memories the way Emma had. She might be nothing more than a footnote in his past life. According to Maeve, he sounded like an entirely different person than the boy Emma had known.

The fact that Emma had chosen to settle in Silver Glen permanently had more to do with the town's charm than it did with Aidan. But her initial motive remained. Even if her apology meant nothing to him, it would clear her own soul of lingering regret.

She couldn't control his response. In fact, he might not even show up. But if he did, she was determined to do the mature, responsible thing and own up to her mistakes.

Emma wanted to grill her visitor, but she had already overstepped the bounds of polite curiosity. "I'm sure he realizes how important it is."

Maeve gathered herself visibly. "You haven't given me an answer. And I warn you in advance that I'll only accept a yes."

"Then I will say yes with pleasure." And a healthy dose of trepidation.

"That's wonderful, Emma dear. My invitation is selfish actually. Everything you say in that delightful British accent makes me want to listen to you for hours, but I have to fly."

"I'd say *you're* the one who has the accent," Emma teased. "You, and the rest of Silver Glen. I've practiced my drawl, but it never seems to come out right."

Heading out the door, Maeve shook her head, laughing. "Let's face it, Emma. You're the quintessential blue-blooded Englishwoman. Fit to marry a prince if Kate hadn't snatched him up first. If you had a slow-as-molasses speech pattern, no one would ever believe you were an aristocrat."

In the sudden silence created by the departure of her vivacious guest, Emma felt her stomach curl. She had known this day would come eventually. It was a major reason she had chosen to roost in Silver Glen. That, and the fact that the town reminded her of the cheery Cotswolds village where she had grown up.

Sooner or later, Aidan would appear. If not at Christmas, then in the spring. The thought of seeing him face-to-face both elated and terrified her. She knew they were far beyond second chances. Too much time had passed. His life experiences had no doubt changed him, especially the tragedy to which Maeve alluded. Too many turns in the road. But Emma wanted to speak her piece. And she would make him listen.

He deserved to know that she had loved him beyond reason and sanity. That his leaving had nearly destroyed her.

Perhaps she was kidding herself. Aidan might not even remember her. Maybe she had magnified the importance of their university romance. Aidan had come to Oxford the fall semester of his senior year for a term-abroad experience. He had literally bumped into Emma on the street in front of a pub frequented by students.

They had both laughed and picked up their books and papers. Aidan offered to buy her dinner, and that was that.

Her heart actually clenched in her chest, the pain of

the memories still fresh after all this time. Would he look the same? Would he think she had changed?

And what was she going to say to Aidan Kavanagh when she saw him again?

Two

Aidan braked carefully and rolled to a stop in front of the courthouse that reigned over the town square. Darkness had fallen swiftly, proof that they were nearing the shortest day of the year. All around him, buildings were decorated in lights…some twinkling white, some a rainbow of colors.

New York City loved to deck itself out for Christmas. But nothing about Christmas in the city was as disturbing as this. As if it were yesterday, he remembered Danielle's delight when he first brought her home to spend the holidays with his family. She had loved the decorations, the town itself and the fresh snow that had fallen.

At least this year the roads were dry. Even so, the image of a long-ago snowball fight brought a small smile to his lips. Danielle had approached everything about her life with the enthusiasm of a puppy.

He was surprised and grateful to find that at least a few memories of their last days together were good ones.

Glancing at his watch, he knew he had lingered long enough. Though Dylan and Mia had invited him to stay with them, Aidan preferred the privacy of a hotel room up at the lodge. Then, it was nobody's business if he couldn't sleep.

His mother had a nice condo in town, though his oldest sibling, Liam, still had a suite with his wife, Zoe, at the Silver Beeches Lodge. They were in the process of designing and building their dream home, but it wouldn't be finished until the following summer.

Liam would be sleeping with one eye open, waiting to make sure that Aidan showed up safely, even if it *was* almost 3:00 a.m. *Why can't you fly down here like a normal person?* he had complained.

Aidan wondered that himself. The grueling hours on the road were supposed to have prepared him for his upcoming ordeal. Well, hell, that was a little too melodramatic. It wasn't as if he hadn't been back to Silver Glen time and again after Danielle was gone. But only once at Christmas. And then only to see his brother in the hospital and make sure he was okay. A little fruitcake, a few packages and as quickly as he could manage, he had returned to his home in New York.

This trip, however, there would be no reprieve. Maeve had already warned him that she expected his presence at an assortment of events and activities. Her third son had strayed beyond her reach, and since she had wrangled his presence via the unexpected wedding invitation, she planned to make the most of it.

Aidan put the car in gear again and cruised around town slowly, expecting at any moment for a cop to pull him over and demand an explanation for his nocturnal prowl. Things looked much the same as they had during his last visit. Except that his brother Dylan's pride and joy, the Silver Dollar Saloon, was once again open for business.

When Aidan had come home for the long 4th of July weekend, the Silver Dollar was still being repaired and renovated after a fire in June. Fortunately, no one had been injured, but he'd heard more than one person bemoaning the fact that the town's most popular watering hole was closed indefinitely.

He looped back toward the square, passing Silver Screen, the community's one and only movie theater. Way back in the forties and fifties, someone had decided all the stores in Silver Glen should be named with the theme of silver. As a marketing ploy, it was brilliant.

The town had grown and prospered, drawing visitors and business from all over the country. Despite his unease, Aidan found himself feeling distinctly nostalgic for this charming valley that had been his home for twenty-plus years.

As he turned the car one last time and headed for the narrow road that would take him up the mountain to the lodge, his headlights flashed across a darkened storefront that didn't look familiar. Silver Memories. From what he could see of the window display, the merchandise appeared to be antiques.

He frowned, almost positive that the last time he'd visited, this particular spot had been a leather shop. Operated by an ornery old guy who made saddles and guitar straps to order.

Odd. But then again, at Thanksgiving, he'd been in town barely twenty-four hours.

When he made it up the mountain, he pulled onto the flagstone apron in front of the Silver Beeches Lodge. After grabbing his bag and handing off his keys to a sleepy parking attendant, he sent a text to his brother. I'm here. Go to bed, old man. See you tomorrow.

A neatly uniformed employee checked him in. After that, it was a matter of minutes to make it onto the elevator, up to the top floor, down the hall and into his quiet, dark, pleasantly scented room.

He kicked off his shoes, plugged in his phone and

fell facedown across the bed, prepared to sleep until someone forced him to get up.

Emma kept one eye on her customer and the other on her laptop. The elderly woman came in a couple of times a month, mostly to window-shop. She actually sold Emma a few items from time to time, clearly in need of cash to supplement her social security check.

Since the white-haired lady seemed content to browse, Emma refocused her attention on the website she'd been perusing. Catriona's Closet was a designer boutique in London that had been Emma's go-to spot for special occasion clothes when she still lived in England. Fortunately for Emma, the shop now boasted a strong online retail presence.

Trying to decide between a cream lace duster over a burgundy long-sleeved jersey dress, or a more traditional green velvet cocktail number with a low, scooped neck, was impossible. With a few quick clicks, she bought them both, with express shipping. If she were going to see Aidan face-to-face, she needed armor. Lots of it. From the cradle, she had been taught the finer points of social etiquette. Mingling socially with the well-regarded and diverse Kavanagh family would pose no threat to her confidence.

But seeing Aidan again? That was another matter.

Finally, the customer left without buying so much as an embroidered hankie. Emma sighed. Her father, if he had lived, would have been horrified at his only daughter stooping to something as bourgeois as *trade*.

The Braithwaites were solicitors and clergymen and physicians, at least the menfolk. The females generally presided over tea, rode to hounds and threw dinner parties, leaving their offspring to be raised by nannies.

Emma had been eight years old before she understood that her dear Baba was not a member of the family.

Shaking off the bittersweet memories, she prepared to close the shop. This time of year, business fell off in the afternoons despite the holidays, so she rarely stayed open past four o'clock.

Outside, people hurried about their errands, braced against the stiff wind and the swirling flurries of snow. Emma would have much preferred to go upstairs to her cozy apartment and snuggle under an afghan, but she was completely out of milk, and she couldn't abide her tea without it.

Bundling into her heavy, raspberry-pink wool coat, she wrapped a black-and-pink scarf around her head, tucked her billfold and keys into her pocket and walked quickly down the street.

At the next block she shivered, impatient for the light to turn green so she could cross the street. So intent was she on making it to the other side that she didn't notice the silver Accord running the light until it was too late.

Her heart beat sluggishly, everything easing into slow motion as she hopped back. But not before the reckless driver clipped her hip, sending her tumbling airborne for several long seconds and then crashing into unforgiving pavement.

Though she was aware of people crowding around her, she lost herself somewhere internally as she catalogued all the places that hurt madly. Teeth chattering, she forced herself to sit up. Nothing appeared to be broken. A man crouched beside her, his scent a mix of warm male, cold air and an oddly familiar cologne.

"Don't move," he said, his honey-toned voice sharp with command.

She was glad to accept his support behind her shoul-

ders. The world swam dizzily. Vaguely, she heard the
wail of sirens.

Shortly after that, brisk strangers loaded her onto a
gurney and lifted her into an ambulance. Though she pro-
tested as much as she was able, no one seemed prepared
to listen to her. Her scarf had slid halfway over one eye.
She was fairly certain her leg was bleeding.

The EMTs wasted no time. The vehicle moved swiftly,
cutting in and out of traffic. Closing her eyes, Emma
winced as a pothole caused fresh discomfort. Fortunately,
the hospital was not far away. Before she knew it, she
had been whisked inside and tucked into an emergency
room cubicle. The dizziness was getting worse. She had
enough presence of mind remaining to wonder if she was
in any kind of serious danger.

A nurse came in to get vitals. Suddenly, the same
deep voice with the bark of command sounded nearby.
"How is she?"

"She's conscious. We'll have to get her up to X ray."

"I'm fine," Emma stated, her determination diluted
somewhat by the high, wavering condition of her voice.

The nurse left. Though Emma's eyes were closed, she
sensed the man standing nearby. His presence had a nar-
cotic effect. She felt safe…as if he were keeping an eye
on things.

"Don't go to sleep," he snapped. "Let's get this damned
scarf out of your face."

She felt him untie it and draw it free. And then he
cursed. "What the hell? Emma?"

She struggled up on one elbow and stared at her white
knight. Instantly, shock flooded her already compromised
nervous system. *Oh, God.* "Aidan. I didn't realize it was
you. Thanks for helping me. I'm sure everything is okay.

You can leave now." The words tripped over each other as her limbs began to shake.

He'd gone white, his eyes wide with what appeared to be a combination of disbelief and horror. "What are you doing here?"

A smile was beyond her. Tears threatened to fall, but she blinked them back. This was not how she'd imagined seeing him again. Not like this. Not without warning. She swallowed hard. "I live here," she whispered.

"The hell you say. Is this some kind of a joke?"

The outrage in his voice and on his face might have been tinged with a hint of panic.

His fury was one blow too many. With a whimper of surrender, she fell back onto the exam table as the world went black…

Aidan strode out of the hospital at a pace little less than full-blown retreat. His heart slugged in his chest and his hands were ice-cold. Of course, that might have been the weather. He'd left his gloves in the car.

Emma was here. And Danielle was not. *Emma*. He repeated her name in his head, still seeing the look of dazed comprehension that filled her wide-set gentian-blue eyes. He was very familiar with those beautiful eyes. Not to mention the porcelain skin, the perfectly curved pink lips, the patrician features, and the silky, fine blond hair that fell past her shoulders. Emma…Good Lord.

The buzzing in his ears was probably a factor of the wind. But then again, his blood pressure might be in the danger zone. His emotions were all over the map. And how ironic was that? He'd made a science of becoming the superficial guy with *no* real emotions.

The lie had been practiced so deeply and so well, he'd begun to believe it himself. But a chance encounter on

the street had cut to the heart of his charade. He was injured, bleeding deep in his gut, raw with pain.

Yet Emma was the one in the hospital.

He had no obligation to go back inside. He'd done his
part. She was in the hands of professionals.

Standing beside his car, he slammed a fist on the
hood…hard enough to bruise his fingers. He'd known
that coming home at Christmas would be a test of how
well he had healed from the past. But never in a million years had he imagined a confrontation with Emma
Braithwaite. She was supposed to be in England, happily married to Viscount Supercilious. Raising upper-
crust rug rats with Harry Potter accents and carelessly
chic clothes.

Damn, damn, damn…

What would happen if he merely walked away? If he
didn't ask for explanations? Could he pretend that the last
two hours were a dream? Or a nightmare?

Another ambulance zipped into the admitting area.
The flashing lights and ear-piercing siren shocked him
back to sanity. He'd left Emma passed out on the exam
table. True, he'd notified a nurse immediately, but after
that he had fled. What would his brothers think if they
could see him now?

They already teased him about his city polish and his
propensity for take-out every night of the week. Even
Liam, who dressed as befitted his position as co-owner
of the prestigious Silver Beeches Lodge, was most at
home clambering about in the mountains. He'd already
taken Zoe camping and made a new convert.

The Kavanagh brothers, out of necessity, were physi-
cally and mentally tough. You didn't grow up with six
same-sex siblings and not learn how to handle yourself
in a fight. But as much as Aidan loved his brothers, he

had always felt a bit out of step with them. He'd wanted to travel the world. He'd been strangled by the small-town lifestyle.

Regardless of the differences in personality and temperament, though, Maeve Kavanagh had taught her sons about responsibility and honor. Perhaps because their father had been lacking in that area, the lessons had stuck. Only the worst kind of cad would leave a woman alone in a hospital with no one to look after her.

Cursing beneath his breath, Aidan gulped in a lungful of icy air. This couldn't be happening. What terrible sins had he committed in the past that karma was so very ready now to kick his ass?

Minutes passed. All around him, people came and went. Hospital staff heading home for the night. Visitors walking toward the doors with worried faces. Aidan barely noted their presence.

Though it shamed him to admit it, he was actually terrified to go back inside. What if Emma were badly hurt? What if even now she was slipping into a coma?

As if it were yesterday he remembered pacing the halls of this very same hospital while Danielle struggled to live. It was a lifetime ago, but the agony was fresh and real. As if it were happening all over again.

He wouldn't allow that. Not on his watch. He had no clue why Emma was in Silver Glen. It didn't matter. He would make sure she was okay, and then he would walk away.

Just like he'd been forced to do ten years ago…

Three

Emma moved her shoulders and moaned. "My head hurts," she whispered. When she tried to focus her eyes, rectangular ceiling tiles above her bed marched from one side of the room to the other. For some reason, that drunken motion made her think of the intricately plastered frieze in her childhood bedroom. She remembered trying to count the individual roses on days when she was ill in bed and stuck at home.

Sadly, this generic space was not nearly as beautiful.

At some point, an unknown set of hands had replaced her clothing with a standard issue hospital gown. The warm blanket tucked up around her shoulders should have felt comforting, but instead, she found it claustrophobic.

Despite her discomfort, she shifted until both arms were free.

An older nurse with kind eyes patted her hand. "You have a concussion. Try not to upset yourself. The pain meds will be kicking in any moment now."

"How long was I out?" She could swear she had only closed her eyes for a moment.

"Not terribly long. But enough for us to get a couple of X rays. They were concerned about your leg, but nothing is broken. You'll have to have a few stitches on your cheek and shin, but that's not too bad considering what might have happened."

"Oh…good…" Someone must have pumped wonderful drugs into her IV, because even with the pain, she was floating on a cloud of worry-free lassitude. Something important nagged at the corners of her mind, but she didn't have the clarity to summon it.

Time passed. Perhaps minutes or hours. She had no clue. She was aware of drifting in and out. Surely it must be dinnertime by now, but she had no appetite.

At one point she was startled by a loud crash in the hallway. Turning her head toward the window, she noted that it was dark. How odd. She remembered heading toward the supermarket for milk. And though the details were fuzzy, she recalled the accident.

But after that things blurred.

When she awoke the next time, her body rebelled. Turning her head, she gagged and reached for the button to summon help. The woman came instantly, offered a basin and spoke soothingly as Emma emptied the contents of her stomach.

The nurse's scrubs were covered in Christmas trees and snowmen. "It's normal, I'm afraid," she said. "The medicine helps the pain, but some people don't tolerate it very well. Try to sleep."

She lowered the lights again and the door swished shut. Feeling dreadfully alone and miserable, Emma was no longer able to stem the flow of tears. She sobbed quietly.

A warm hand stroked her hair. "Hush, Emma. Don't cry. Go back to sleep."

Her eyelids felt weighted down. But she forced them open for long enough to make out the shape of a man seated in a chair beside her bed. "Aidan? I thought I dreamed you."

His laugh sounded rusty, as if he hadn't used it in a while. "I'm afraid not."

"Why are you here?" The syllables slurred together. She was so very tired.

Still he stroked her hair. "It doesn't matter. You're going to be okay. Go to sleep."

When she awoke toward morning, her brain was clearer, but her body felt as if she had gone three rounds with a professional boxer. Maybe the medicine was worth it after all.

In one surreptitious glance, she ascertained that the room was empty. The taste of disappointment filled her mouth. Perhaps Aidan had been a dream after all.

An aide came in with breakfast. Emma's stomach flopped sickeningly at the scent of scrambled eggs, but the tea bag on the tray caught her attention. When the woman arranged the rolling table across Emma's lap and raised the head of the bed, Emma thought she might be sick again.

Breathing deeply, she closed her eyes and remained perfectly still until the feeling passed. At last, she summoned the energy to brew a life-saving cup of Earl Grey. With a dash of sugar, a squirt of lemon and a dollop of artificial creamer, the result was not entirely acceptable, but it was better than nothing.

She was poking at a lumpy biscuit when a female physician entered the room. "Ms. Braithwaite. How are you feeling?"

Emma shrugged. "Like I was hit by something big and hard?"

The doctor grinned. "Aptly put. We've patched you up,

and all your stats are good. Don't get me wrong. You're going to be in bad shape for a few days. But you were very lucky. It could have been a lot worse. I'm thinking of releasing you later today once I see how you do with your meals. Is there anyone at home who can look after you? So you don't have to be on your feet too much?"

Emma opened her mouth to speak, but before she could answer, a man stepped from the hallway into the room. "I'll get her settled and make sure she has help."

Aidan. She couldn't have been any more surprised if the Loch Ness Monster had paraded down the hall. Apparently the sexy phantom in her dreams was entirely real.

"That won't be necessary," she said firmly. Even as she spoke, she scrambled mentally for other alternatives.

Mia would be willing to lend a hand, but she had a baby to care for and a wedding to plan. And Emma definitely was not going to ask Aidan's mother for help. Which left Mrs. Correll, the retired lady who worked part-time at the antique store. But the older woman battled arthritis and couldn't climb stairs.

Emma hadn't lived in Silver Glen all that long. Certainly not long enough to have an extensive list of friends on hand to provide casseroles and sympathy soup.

Aidan ignored Emma's protest. He gave the white-coated physician a high-wattage smile that made her blink twice. "I'll make sure she follows your orders exactly, Doctor. You can count on me."

The doctor departed. Emma stared at the man who once upon a time had been her knight in shining armor. "I can explain," she said, eager to clear the air.

Aidan held up a hand, his gaze wintry. "I don't want to hear anything about the past or why you're here. I'm not interested, Emma. I'm going to take you home and sleep on your couch overnight. But that's it. I have no desire to hear anything you have to say. Are we clear?"

Her heart sank. She had hoped his animosity might have dwindled after all this time. But, no. She was an unwelcome obligation to him. Nothing more. Not even worth the effort of polite conversation.

Her throat tight, she nodded. Though it pained her to admit it, she didn't have the luxury of arguing with him. If Aidan's assurances of aid were enough to get her dismissed from the hospital, then she would swallow the words that wanted to tumble forth in a plea for understanding.

She watched him focus his gaze on the muted television as he feigned great interest in an infomercial for egg separators. His profile was dear and familiar, but the boy she had once known was gone, replaced by a man with even broader shoulders and a physique that was honed and strong.

His dark brown hair with a hint of red was expertly cut, his clothing masculine and expensive. The young university student she remembered had flaunted shaggy locks and a succession of rock-and-roll T-shirts that showcased his flat abdomen. Close-fitting denims had outlined long legs and a tight butt. His grin and American accent won over every girl in a ten-mile radius. But at the end of the day, he went home to Emma's off-campus apartment.

Shaking off the poignant memories, she stared at him. He'd said *no explanations*, so what else was there to talk about?

Abruptly, he turned to face her. "I'll ask the nurses' station to call me when they're ready to dismiss you. In the meantime, I have errands to run."

And with that, he was gone.

* * *

Emma ate and drank and did everything that was asked of her. For one panicked hour she contemplated faking a relapse to avoid being alone with the painfully distant man who looked so much like the Aidan Kavanagh she had once known. But as much as she dreaded being beholden to the glacial-eyed Aidan, she also wanted to get out of this noisy hospital and back into her own bed.

After a long afternoon of additional tests and X rays and blood work, a physician's assistant showed up and announced that Emma was free to go. Aidan appeared just as she tried standing beside the bed to dress in her sadly damaged street clothes.

He cursed quietly. "For God's sake. You're going to fall over." Her tights were badly torn. Aidan took one look at them and tossed them in the trash. "You'll have to go bare-legged on the way home," he said, "but I assume you live close?"

She nodded, humiliated by the way he tucked and pulled and fastened her bits and pieces as if she were a helpless child. Tension radiated from his large frame. Her head pounded, but she was damned if she would show weakness in front of this brusque stranger.

When her few belongings were gathered and in her lap, an orderly eased her into a wheelchair and gave Aidan a nod. "If you'll bring your car around to the front entrance, sir, I'll meet you there with Ms. Braithwaite."

Aidan nodded and vanished.

Emma wouldn't have minded a tour of the hospital, or a quick peek at the maternity ward with all the brand-new babies. Anything to postpone the moment of truth.

If she hadn't been in so much pain, physical and mental, the pun might have made her smile. Aidan didn't *want* to hear the truth. He'd already judged her and found her guilty. He believed that she had betrayed his trust. In his defense, the evidence had been pretty damning.

Outside, the wind was no less biting than it had been the day before. Only now it was dark as well. By the time she sank into the passenger seat of Aidan's fancy sports car with the heated leather seats, she was shivering. He grabbed a jacket from the backseat and handed it to her.

"Wrap that around your legs." He paused, staring out the windshield. His granite jaw flexed. "I need your address."

She sensed that having to ask for that one small piece of information pissed him off. Muttering the street and number, she leaned back and closed her eyes. The car smelled like him. Maybe he would let her sleep here. The prospect of making it all the way to her bed was daunting to say the least.

He parked at the curb in front of her business, his hands clenched on the wheel. "Here?" he asked, incredulity in his voice.

"I have an apartment upstairs. You don't need to stay. Really."

Ignoring her statement completely, he half turned in his seat and fixed her with a steady gaze that left her feeling naked…and not in a good way. The hazel eyes that had once twinkled with good humor were flat. It was difficult to believe that *anything* about this older, tougher Aidan twinkled.

His jaw worked. "Correct me if I'm wrong, but I was under the impression that Lady Emma Braithwaite was an heiress. To the tune of several million pounds. I can't fathom why she would be here in the mountains of North Carolina running an antiques shop when she grew up in a damned castle." He was practically shouting at the end.

"It wasn't a castle." His sarcasm cut deep, but it also made her angry. "You said you didn't want any explanations," she reminded him. "If you don't mind, I'm very tired and I need to take some medicine. If you'll help me up the stairs, you can go." She managed an even-toned, reasonable response until her voice broke on the last word. Biting down hard on her bottom lip, she swallowed and inhaled the moment of weakness.

After several long, pregnant seconds, Aidan muttered something inaudible and got out, slamming his door hard enough to rattle the window beside her. Before she could brace herself for what came next, he opened her side of the car and leaned in to scoop her into his arms.

She shrank back instinctively, unwilling to get any closer. He stumbled when her quick movement threw him off balance. "Put your arm around my neck, Emma. Before I drop you." Irritation accented every syllable.

"Are you always so grumpy?" she asked. If anyone had cause to be out of sorts, it was she.

He locked the car with the key fob and settled her more firmly into his embrace. "Don't push it."

To the left of her storefront, a single narrow door gave entrance to a steep flight of steps. The building dated back to the early days of Silver Glen. When Aidan took the key from her and let himself in, she wondered if his big frame would make it up the stairwell, especially carrying her.

But he was a natural athlete. She never even felt a jostle or a bump as he ascended to the second floor and her quaint apartment. His chest and his arms were hard, though he carried her carefully. If it were possible, she thought she might get drunk on the scent of his skin and the faint starchy smell of his crisp cotton shirt.

A second door at the top required a key as well. By

now, Aidan should have been breathing heavily. Emma was five-eight and not a slip of a woman. But he managed the final hurdle and kicked open the door, reaching with one hand to turn on the light.

She knew the exact moment he spotted her sofa. The red, velvet-covered Victorian settee was designed more for looks than for comfort. It was definitely not meant for sleeping. Fortunately, she owned a more traditional chair and ottoman that were tucked up close to her gas-log fireplace. If Aidan were determined to spend the night, he would be under no illusions as to his accommodations.

The apartment was fairly warm. When she'd left the day before, she had only been nipping out to grab the milk, intending to return in little more than a half hour. That was a blessing. If the rooms had been ice-cold as they sometimes were, her misery would have been complete.

He set her on her feet in the bedroom, not even glancing at her large brass bed with its intensely feminine white lace sheets and comforter. "Can you get ready for the night on your own?" His hands remained on her shoulders, though it was clear he was lending physical support, nothing more.

"Of course." Her right leg felt as if someone had delved into it with an ax, and her head was a heartbeat away from a painful explosion, but she'd die before she would admit it. She had been brought up not to make a fuss. Her father hadn't liked female *histrionics*, as he called them.

Aidan stared down at her. For the first time, she saw something in his eyes that told her the past might be gone, but it was not forgotten. For the space of one brief, heart-stopping breath, she was sure she witnessed tenderness. But it vanished in an instant…perhaps never there to begin with. He unbuttoned her bedraggled coat and eased it from her shoulders.

"Where are your pajamas?" he asked.

She wrapped her arms around her waist. "I'll get them. Go fix yourself a cup of coffee."

One eyebrow lifted. "You have coffee?"

In England, she had done her best to wean him from the uncivilized beverage. "For guests," she said stiffly.

He nodded once and walked away. Sinking down onto the bed, she told herself she could manage to wash up and change clothes. It was a matter of pride and self-preservation. Having Aidan help was unthinkable. She was far too aware of him as it was. His physical presence dwarfed her cozy apartment.

In the bathroom she dared to glance in the mirror and groaned. Why had no one seen fit to give her a hairbrush? Moving as carefully as an old lady, she removed her rumpled and stained blouse and skirt and stripped off her undies and bra. Bruises already marked her skin in a dozen places. She had been given strict instructions not to get her stitches wet, so a shower was out. With a soft washcloth and a bar of her favorite lavender soap, she managed a quick cleanup.

When she was done, she realized that she had forgotten to get a nightgown from the bureau. Wrapping a towel around herself sarong-style, she opened the bathroom door and walked into the bedroom.

As she did so, she caught Aidan leaning down to put a cup of steaming hot tea on her bedside table.

Four

Aidan froze. If Emma's eyes grew any bigger, they would eclipse her face. Though it hurt to look at her, he forced himself to meet her gaze with dispassion. "Drink your tea while it's hot," he said. "I'll see what I can whip up for our dinner."

In her tiny kitchen, he put his hands on the table, palms flat, and bowed his head. So many feelings, so many memories...

Emma laughed up at him, her skin dappled by shadows from the willow tree that served as shelter for their impromptu picnic. "Why the serious look?" she asked.

She lay on her back, arms outstretched above her head, eyes ripe with happiness. They had borrowed an old quilt from her neighbor. The faded colors only made her more beautiful in comparison.

"I have to go home soon," he said, unable to comprehend the upcoming rift. "What will I do without you?" He sat upright, his back propped against the tree trunk, trying not to think about how much he wanted to make love to her at this moment. But the perfectly manicured English park was filled with adults and children eager to enjoy the warmth of a late fall afternoon.

Emma linked her fingers with his, pulling his hand to her lips. "Don't spoil it," she whispered, for a moment seeming as desperately dejected as he was. But immediately, her optimism returned, even if manufactured. "Remember—you'll graduate in the spring, and then we'll have all sorts of choices."

There was no acceptable choice if it didn't include her. He managed a grimace that was supposed to placate her. But from the expression on her face, he knew she saw through him. She had since the first day they met.

He lay down at her side, not caring if anyone raised an eyebrow. Propped on an elbow, he brushed the back of his hand down her cheek. "I can't leave you, Emma. I can't..."

But in the end, he had...

Inhaling sharply, he slammed the door on recollections that served no purpose. That day was so far in the past, it might as well be written up in the history books. Perhaps in a chapter labeled "youthful indiscretions."

Turning his attention to practical matters, he examined the contents of Emma's fridge. The woman lived on yogurt and granola and fancy cheese. His stomach rumbled in protest. But he'd have to make do with a gourmet grilled cheese sandwich.

He found a skillet and spooned a dollop of butter into it, listening to the sizzle as he strained to hear movement in Emma's room. Even now, the image of her half-naked body remained imprinted on his brain. All that creamy English skin. Long legs. Hair the color of spring sunshine.

He dropped a chunk of cheese on the burner and had to fish it out before he set off the smoke alarm. His final efforts were not visually pleasing, but the sandwiches would keep them both from starving.

Leaving his meal in the kitchen, he took Emma's plate to her door and knocked quietly. She would be dressed by now, but he didn't want any additional surprises. He knocked a second time and then opened the door a crack. "Emma?"

The lights were on, but Emma was in bed, fast asleep. Curled on her side, she slept like a child with a hand under her cheek. A neat row of stitches near her ear reminded him anew of how close she had come to disaster.

He glanced at his watch. He hated to wake her, but if she awoke later in pain, it would be worse. He put the plate on the dresser and crouched beside the bed. The instinct to touch her was one he had to ignore.

"Emma," he said quietly, not wanting to startle her.

She moved restlessly but didn't open her eyes.

"Emma."

This time her eyelids fluttered. A small smile curved her lips before she realized where she was and with whom. Immediately, a mask slipped over her features. "Aidan. I told you to go. I'll sleep 'til morning."

Fishing the bottle of pills out of his pocket, he shook a couple of tablets into his palm. "The doctor gave you enough pain meds to last until we can get your prescription filled tomorrow. You're an hour past due, so you'd better take them. And at least eat a few bites of food."

She took his offering with visible reluctance and washed it down with two sips of tea. When he brought the grilled cheese, she stared at it. "You cooked for me?"

He felt his face redden. His lack of expertise in the kitchen was well documented. "It's a sandwich," he said gruffly. "Don't get too excited. I'll be back in a minute with a glass of milk. That might help you sleep."

When he returned, she had managed to finish half of the meal. He held out the tumbler of milk and waited until she drained most of it. Already, the simple exertion of eating had taxed her strength. She was as pale as her bedding, and he saw her hands shake before she tucked them beneath the sheets and settled back into her original position.

"Do you want the lights off?" he asked.

"I suppose. Please leave, Aidan."

He flipped off all except the bathroom light. Leaving that door cracked an inch or so, he took one last look at the patient. "Go to sleep. Everything will be better in the morning."

The chair and ottoman were more comfortable than they appeared. With the gas logs flickering and a couple of woolen throws in lieu of blankets, he managed to fall asleep. His dreams were a mishmash of good and bad, past and present.

Somewhere in the middle of the night a crash jerked him out of his restless slumber. Leaping to his feet, he headed for Emma's room, almost sure the noise had emanated from that direction.

He found her in the bathroom surrounded by the broken remains of a small water glass she kept on the counter. "Don't move," he barked. Her feet were bare. Scooping her up, he avoided the worst of the mess and carried her back to bed. "Why didn't you call me?" he grumbled.

"I didn't need a witness for *that*," she snapped. Even drugged and injured, she had spunk.

Smothering a smile he knew she wouldn't appreciate, he tucked her in and straightened the covers. It was still another forty-five minutes before she could have anything for pain. "How do you feel?"

She shrugged, her expression mulish. "How do you think?"

Evidently, the ladylike manners were eroding in direct proportion to her unhappiness. "Sorry I asked," he said drolly, hoping to coax a smile.

But Emma turned her back on him. "Don't be here when I wake up," she ordered, the words pointed.

He shook his head though she couldn't see him. "Do you want me to bring in the medicine when it's time?"

"No." She burrowed her face into her arm. "I can take care of myself."

Emma had cause to regret her hasty words only a few hours later. When pale winter sunshine peeked into her room, she stirred and groaned. Today was worse than yesterday, and that was saying something. Of course, part of the problem was her stubborn pride. It was long past time for a pain pill, and she was paying the price.

She eased onto her back and listened. The apartment was silent and still. For a moment, she panicked about the shop, and then she remembered it was Sunday. Well, she wasn't going to get any relief until she took something, so she had to get out of this bed.

Cursing softly when pain shot up her thigh, she grabbed hold of the foot rail and found her balance. Her slippers were tucked beneath the edge of the bed, but if she bent to retrieve them, she was fairly certain her headache would ratchet upward about a million notches.

Tiptoeing on icy feet, she went in search of the elusive pill bottle. What she found was Aidan, sleeping soundly beside the hearth. Her shock was equal parts relief and dismay. His longs legs sprawled across her ottoman, his shoes in a jumble nearby. Though his neck was bent at an awkward angle, he snored softly, irrefutable evidence that he was actually slumbering.

She counted the breaths as his broad chest rose and fell. Though she couldn't see his eyes, she knew their color by heart. Hazel, beautiful irises that changed with his mood. Lately all she had seen was the dark glare of disapproval.

His thick hair was mussed. The top three buttons of his shirt were undone, revealing a dusting of hair below his collarbone. The intimacy of the scene curled her stomach with regret and sharp envy. No doubt there was a woman in New York who had laid claim to this beautiful man. But Emma had known him before…before he had acquired the spit and polish of a successful entrepreneur.

As he slumbered, she finally caught a glimpse of the boy she had known. After all, even at twenty-one she and Aidan had been little more than teenagers. They'd had no clue what forces could tear them apart, no way to understand that life seldom produced fairy-tale endings.

The old Emma would have curled into his embrace, not waiting for an invitation, confident of her welcome. Wistfully, she allowed herself a full minute to watch him sleep. But no more.

Easing past him, she spied the bottle on the end table, scooped it up and retreated before the lion awoke and caught her gawking at him. Her bravery extended only so far.

Though she would sell her soul for a cup of hot tea, that luxury would have to wait. The simple task was more than she could handle at the moment, and she had leaned on Aidan far too much already.

Thankfully, he never stirred as she retraced her steps. The partial glass of milk from the night before still sat beside her bed. It wouldn't have spoiled in this amount of time, and she needed something to coat her stomach. Wrinkling her nose at the taste, she swallowed the medicine with one big gulp of liquid.

Though she had heard Aidan clean up the mess in

the bathroom, she knew it was foolhardy to go in there again with bare feet. So she forced herself to slowly and carefully retrieve her footwear from its hiding place beneath the bed. When she straightened, she saw black spots dancing in front of her eyes and her forehead was clammy.

Even so, her immediate need was pressing. After a quick visit to the facilities, she washed her face, brushed her teeth and shuffled back to bed. She didn't even bother glancing at the clock. What did it matter? She had no place to go.

Aidan breathed a sigh of relief when he heard Emma's door shut. He'd heard her the moment she climbed out of bed. Feigning sleep had seemed the wisest course of action. But he hadn't anticipated how strongly her silent perusal would affect him.

What was she thinking as she stood there and stared at him? How did she reconcile the way they had left things between them years ago with her current choice to live in Silver Glen? She had to possess an agenda. There was no way she could call such a thing coincidence. She was far too intelligent to try that tactic.

The only explanation was that she had come here intentionally. But why?

He told himself it didn't matter. And he almost believed it.

Scraping his hands through his hair, he sat up and put on his shoes. As he rolled his neck trying to undo the kinks, he wondered how long it had been since he'd spent a platonic night on a woman's sofa.

Emma would probably sleep for a few hours now that she had taken her medicine. Which meant he had time to drop off her prescription, grab some breakfast and dash up to the hotel for clean clothes and a shower.

The first two items on his list were accomplished without incident. But when he tried to access the back stairs at the Silver Beeches to avoid any awkward questions, he ran in to Liam coming down as he was going up.

His older brother, dressed to the nines as always, lifted an eyebrow. "Look what the cat dragged in."

"Don't rag on me, Liam. I haven't slept worth a damn."

"At least not in your own bed. I thought all your lady friends were in New York."

Aidan counted to ten and then to twenty. Liam was not giving him any more grief than usual, but Aidan wasn't in the mood to be teased. Not today. His jaw clenched, he offered a simple explanation, knowing that Liam wouldn't let him pass without at least that. "I ran in to a friend who was having a bit of trouble. I helped out. That's all. Now if you don't mind, I'd like to go to my room and get cleaned up."

Liam leaned against the wall, his arms crossed over his chest. "This wouldn't have anything to do with the young woman who was hit by a car day before yesterday...downtown?"

Aidan stared at him. "Damn it. That's exactly why I don't live here anymore. Nobody has anything better to do than gossip."

"People were concerned. Silver Glen is a tight-knit place."

"Yeah. I got that."

Liam's face changed, all trace of amusement gone. "I know it's hard for you to be here this time of year. But I want you to know how glad we all are to have you home for the holidays."

The knot in Aidan's chest prevented him from answering—that and the sting of emotion that tightened his throat.

His sibling knew him too well to be fooled. "I'll let you go," Liam said, his eyes expressing the depth of their relationship. "If I can help with anything, let me know."

Five

By the time Aidan picked up the prescription and made it back to Emma's place, almost two hours had passed. He had taken her key with him, so he let himself in quietly and placed his packages on the table. Peeking into the bedroom, he saw that she still slept.

The extra rest was good for her. And besides, the sooner she was stable, the sooner he could leave.

He shoved the carryout bags he had picked up into the fridge. The greasy burgers and fries came from a mom-and-pop joint down the street. The Silver Shake Shack had been there since he was a kid. While Emma had converted Aidan to drinking proper English tea, he had been the one to teach her the joys of comfort food.

His immediate mission accomplished, he sprawled in the chair again and scrolled through his email. No big surprises there. Except for the one from his mother that said: Dinner at eight. S.B. dining room. Don't make me hunt you down.

He laughed softly, knowing that had been her intention. Everyone wanted Aidan to be in a good mood. To be happy. He understood their concern, but he was fine. He was here, wasn't he? They couldn't expect more than that.

Evidently the smell of his lunch offering permeated the apartment. Emma wandered out of her room wearing stretchy black knit pants and a hip-length cashmere sweater. She had done her hair up in a ponytail, and wore bunny slippers on her feet.

She gave him a diffident smile. "Hey."

"Hey, yourself. Doing any better?"

"Actually, yes. Was that food I smelled?"

"Some of the best. I put it in the fridge, but it hasn't been there long. We can zap it in the microwave. Are you hungry now?'

She nodded, heading for her small dining table. Her gait was halting, so he knew her leg was bothering her.

While Emma sat and rested her head in her hands, he managed to rustle up paper plates and condiments. "I ordered you one with mustard, mayo and tomato. I hope that's still the way you like it."

Her expression guarded, she nodded. "Sounds lovely."

The silent meal was half-awkward, half-familiar. Emma had changed very little over the years, though he did see a few fine lines at the corners of her eyes. She had always been more serious than he was, conscientious to a fault. The one thing he couldn't help noticing was that her breasts had filled out. The soft sweater emphasized them and her narrow waist.

When the food was gone, down to the last crumb, he cleared the table. "Do you feel like sitting up for a little while? I'll give you the seat by the fire."

"That would be nice."

So polite. Like a little girl minding her manners. Swallowing his irritation at her meekness, he hovered as she made her way across the room. He wouldn't touch her unless she showed signs of being lightheaded. When she was settled, he stood in the center of the room, hands in his pockets. "If you have an extra key," he said, "I can check on you later and you won't have to get up to answer the door. I have dinner plans, but I'll bring you something hot to eat before I go."

Staring into the fire, she nodded. Her profile, silhouetted against the flames, had the purity of an angel's. He felt something in his chest wrench and pull. The shaft of pain took his breath away. That wouldn't do. Not at all. He was way past dancing to Emma Braithwaite's tune.

He made a show of glancing at his watch. "Will you be okay for the afternoon on your own?"

"Of course." Her chin lifted with all the haughtiness of a duchess.

For all he knew, she might actually *be* a duchess. He hadn't kept up with the details of her life. Anything was possible.

She pointed. "The spare key is in the top drawer of that desk by the window. I think it's tied to a bit of green ribbon."

He rummaged as directed and found what he was looking for. As he pushed everything back into place, his gaze landed on a familiar-looking piece of paper. When he recognized what it was, he felt a mule-kick to the chest. "Emma?"

"Yes?"

He held up the offending card. "Would you care to explain why you have an invitation to my brother's wedding?"

Emma groaned inwardly. Could things get any worse? Aidan's original animosity had faded as he cared for her. Now his suspicions were back in full force. His expression was glacial, his demeanor that of judge and jury combined.

"Your mother gave it to me," she said, the words flat. Let him think what he wanted.

"My mother…"

Emma nodded. "I'm sure Mia asked her to. Mia and I became friends when I moved here a few months ago."

"How convenient."

As bad as she felt, her anger escalated. "I don't know what you're implying, and I don't care. I don't have to explain myself to you. Leave the key and go. I can manage by myself."

His face darkened with some strong emotion as he crushed the beautiful invitation in his fist. "You have no food in the house. I said I would bring your dinner. Now if you'll excuse me, I have things to do."

The way he slammed the door as he walked out was entirely unnecessary. She already knew he was furious. And that was just too damn bad. Emma had as much right to be in Silver Glen as he had. If he cared to listen, she would be happy to explain. But she had a sneaking suspicion that Aidan Kavanagh was too darned stubborn to hear her out.

Aidan wondered if he were losing his mind. Had the trauma of coming to Silver Glen at Christmas finally made him snap? When he left Emma's apartment, he sat downstairs in his car for several long minutes, trying to decide what to do. Finally, he drove out to Dylan's place for a visit. If he should happen to pump Mia for information in the meantime, that was *his* business.

Dylan answered the door, his face lighting up as he grabbed Aidan in a bear hug. "Thanks for coming home, baby brother. It means the world to Mia and me. I couldn't have a wedding without you."

Aidan shrugged, uncomfortable that everyone was making such a big deal of his visit. "Of course I'm here. Why wouldn't I be?"

The empathy in Dylan's steady gaze made Aidan feel raw and vulnerable, neither of which was the least bit appealing to a grown man.

Mia broke the awkward silence. "I'm glad you're here, too. And so is Cora."

Aidan took the child automatically as Mia handed her over. Cora gave him a sweet smile that exposed two tiny front teeth. He kissed her forehead. "Hey, darlin'. You want to go joyriding with Uncle Aidan? I'll show you where all the toddler boys live."

Mia rolled her eyes. "Why is it that no one in the Kavanagh family knows how to talk to girls?"

Dylan looked at her with mock outrage. "I might point out that *you* fell for some of my best lines."

Mia kissed her soon-to-be-husband on the cheek. "Whatever helps you sleep at night…"

Aidan grinned. He'd expected to be a little jealous of Dylan's storybook ending…and Liam's. And perhaps on some level, he was. But even so, he was happy for his older brothers. It was about time the Kavanaghs found something to celebrate.

Reggie Kavanagh had died when his boys were young. Liam, at sixteen, had been the only one close to adulthood. Truthfully, it wasn't exactly accurate to say that Reggie died. One day he simply went off into the mountains and never returned. Looking for the silver mine that had put his ancestors and the town of Silver Glen on the map.

Aidan tried to shake off the memory. He could still see his mother's face at the memorial service. She had been devastated, but resigned. Apparently, Reggie had never been the husband she deserved. But then again, life wasn't about getting what you were owed. It was more about dealing with what you were given.

In Aidan's case, that meant surviving loss. First his father. Then Emma. And finally, poor Danielle.

Cora's pudgy little body was warm and solid in his arms. A baby was such beautiful proof of life's goodness. Aidan needed that reminder now and again. He glanced at his brother, who apparently couldn't resist nibbling his wife's neck since Aidan was running interference with Cora.

Aidan complained. "In case it's escaped your notice, your innocent daughter is right here in front of you. How about a little decorum?"

"Decorum sucks." Dylan grabbed Mia for a quick smacking kiss on the lips. While Mia giggled and turned pink, Aidan put a hand over Cora's face. "Don't look," he whispered. "The adults are being inappropriate."

Laughing, but starry-eyed, Mia rescued her daughter and cuddled her close. "She'd better get used to it. Dylan wants at least two more."

Aidan lifted an eyebrow. "Seriously?" His brother had changed a lot in the last year. He was happier. More grounded. Less defensive about his place in the world.

"I like having kids around." Dylan's crooked grin said he recognized Aidan's astonishment and understood it. There had been a time when Dylan was the ultimate party animal. Now, however, he had embraced the role of family man with enthusiasm.

It didn't hurt that beautiful, quiet, smart-as-Einstein Mia shared his bed every night. They were an unlikely couple in many ways, but somehow the two of them together made it work.

Mia glanced at her watch. "Are you both going up to the lodge to eat with your mom and the rest of the clan?"

"You're not?" Aidan was surprised. His mother's command performances demanded proper deference.

Mia shook her head. "I've been given a dispensation. I want to get Cora to bed on her usual schedule, because we're going to Asheville tomorrow to find her a dress for the wedding."

"Cutting it a little close, aren't you?"

Mia shook her head. "Blame it on your brother. He's the one who decided we had to get married ASAP."

"Because?"

Dylan spoke up, his face a study in love and devotion as he eyed the two women in his house. "I'm adopting Cora," he said. "The papers are going to be finalized the day after Christmas. I want us to be a family before the New Year."

Conversation wandered in less serious directions after that. Dylan offered Aidan a beer while Mia sprawled on the floor to play with Cora. Aidan decided in that quiet half hour that he couldn't go back to Emma's. Not today. He had things to figure out, and he needed space and time to understand what her motives were.

When he and Dylan joined the two females on the floor, Aidan addressed Mia. "I need a favor, since you and Cora aren't going up the mountain for dinner."

She untangled Cora's fingers from her hair. "Name it. I need to build up all the family points I can get."

He chuckled. "It's nothing bad, I swear. But did you hear about the accident in town on Friday afternoon?"

Mia nodded, pausing to blow a raspberry on Cora's tummy. "Someone ran a red light and hit a pedestrian."

"Yes. I happened to be there at the time and followed the ambulance to the hospital. The woman's name is Emma Braithwaite. She says she's friends with you."

He felt a lick of shame at manipulating his sister-in-law. But he needed to know if Emma had disclosed the relationship she shared with Aidan.

Mia's gaze was anxious. "Is she okay?"

He nodded. "Home resting now. A concussion and some stitches. She didn't want to bother you because of the baby and the wedding. But it seems that she's fairly new in town… right? And doesn't know many people? I was hoping you and Cora could run over there and take her some dinner."

Dylan's eyes narrowed as though he sensed something was going on but wasn't sure what. "Who died and made you Clara Barton?"

"I watched the accident happen. All I had in mind was heading to the hospital and making sure she was okay. But when I found out she didn't have anyone to help out, I offered to get her home and settled when she was discharged."

"How convenient."

Hearing Dylan voice the same sarcastic response Aidan had used with Emma made him wince inwardly. "I don't know what you're talking about."

"Give me a break, Aidan. I've seen Emma. She's tall, blond and gorgeous…with a voice like an angel. You were smitten and decided to go all Galahad on her poor, helpless self."

Mia looked up with a frown. "I'm sitting *right* here," she said.

Dylan gave her a smoochy face. "Don't worry, my love. You know I'm into short, dark and cuddly."

"Oh, dear Lord," Aidan groused. "You two are embarrassing little Cora."

Cora, oblivious to the repartee, played with her toes.

Aidan weighed the facts. Clearly, Emma had made no mention to Mia of the fact that Emma and Aidan went way back. So if she wasn't using her past relationship with Aidan to ingratiate herself into the Kavanagh family, what was her deal?

* * *

He wrestled with his suspicions all evening, in the midst of a loud, argumentative, completely normal dinner with his siblings and his mother. To be honest, he'd forgotten how much fun it could be when they were all together. Usually when he came home to visit, at least one or two of the crew were missing…spread out here, there and yonder. It was increasingly difficult to corral all the Kavanaghs in the same place at the same time.

Maeve hadn't forgotten, though. It was at her insistence that they were all gathered under one roof tonight. And this was only the first of a series of holiday moments scripted by the matriarch of the family.

Liam's wife, Zoe—still with a new bride's glow—fit right in. Unlike the introverted Mia, Zoe loved a social gathering. She laughed and flirted and played the role of naive newcomer with verve, all under the indulgent eye of her besotted husband.

Aidan tipped a metaphorical hat to his mom. With Dylan's wedding, the whole Christmas season and a brand-new, soon-to-be-adopted Kavanagh kiddo, Maeve had scored a trifecta.

He left the Silver Beeches Lodge with a smile on his face. Though his room was upstairs, he was too wired to sleep. Instead, he climbed into his car and drove toward town. The closer he came to Emma's place of business, the less he smiled.

Parking at the curb below her windows, he stared up at the light. Why had she come to Silver Glen? He told himself he didn't care, but that was a lie. The Emma he had known in college was neither devious nor vengeful. Though, that was a very long time ago. Had she somehow decided to blame him for the meltdown of their relationship?

Only the most naive of assessments could attribute anything positive to her unexpected appearance in Silver Glen. His immediate reaction to finding her was suspicion and wariness. None of this made sense.

But even knowing that she had made the acquaintance of at least of two of his family members and that she had never once mentioned to either of them her connection to Aidan, he didn't want to believe the worst.

Truthfully, now that he had spent some time with her, it was impossible to hold back the flood of memories. Feelings he thought long dead pumped adrenaline into his bloodstream. She was like a drug in his system. He had detoxed after she nearly ruined his life. But the addiction was still there. Waiting to be resurrected.

If he had an ounce of self-preservation, he would stay the hell away. He'd crafted a decent life for himself—an even-keeled existence with no surprises, no regrets. No highs, no lows. It was safe…and financially remunerative. Even without his share of the family business, he had plenty of disposable income. And many friends of both sexes to help him fritter it away.

Emma's unexpected incursion into his life shouldn't even be a blip on his radar. Yet he had spent the night at her place. The same old Aidan, looking out for a woman who didn't want or need his protection.

He knew better.

But did he have the guts to turn his back on the one person who had taught him both the incredible rush of desire entwined with new love and also the soul-crushing agony of betrayal?

Six

December in the mountains of North Carolina was a capricious season. It could either be snowy and cold, balmy and sunny, or—as was the case this year—wet and gloomy.

Emma leaned against the windowsill, hands tucked in the pockets of her chenille robe, and watched water droplets track down the glass. Her view of the street below was distorted…like an image in a dream.

For four days she had expected Aidan to return, and for four days she had been disappointed. Now, there was no denying the truth. He was not coming back.

Having Mia show up on her doorstep Sunday evening had been the first sign. Though Emma was delighted to see her friend and little Cora, the fact that Aidan had promised to bring her dinner and then delegated that responsibility suggested he had been caring for Emma only out of a sense of duty.

She was the one who had wishfully attributed his emotions to feelings of affection. Which was ludicrous, really…she fully admitted that. Aidan had good reason to despise her. Only the honor and integrity instilled by Maeve Kavanagh into each and every one of her sons had compelled Aidan to come to Emma's aid.

Twitching the lace sheers back into place, she contemplated the outfit that lay draped across the red velvet settee. Tonight was the first of Maeve's holiday events—a fete for Dylan and Mia. Since the wedding plans had been thrown together so quickly, there hadn't been time for a more traditional bridal shower.

Because Dylan's home was fully outfitted, particularly with the addition of Mia's things, tonight's invitation had requested gifts to one of three charities in lieu of toasters and stemware. Emma had already written a large check and tucked it in her shimmery silver clutch. As a small thank-you gift to Mia and Dylan for their friendship, she had wrapped up a memento—an antique silver picture frame engraved on the lower edge with the words, *'til the end of time...*

In her imagination, she saw a young war bride tucking it into her soldier's pocket as he headed off to the other side of the world. Emma was a romantic. And a proud one. At one time, she had believed that every woman could find her soul mate. Now, older and wiser, she wasn't entirely sure. But she still hadn't given up on romance, even if it was mostly for other people.

Quite honestly, she didn't want to go tonight. Her leg still hurt, though it was much improved, and her head ached if she tried to do too much. But the doctor had cleared her to go back to work.

If she planned to open the shop tomorrow after a several-day absence, she could hardly expect Maeve to understand if Emma cried off tonight's festivities for health reasons. She was trapped by her affection for Mia and Maeve and the many kindnesses they had shown her as a newcomer to Silver Glen.

On the upside, if Aidan were avoiding her, it would make tonight more tolerable. Maybe they could sit on opposite sides of the room. She didn't have a problem with that, at all.

She sat down and stroked the fabric of her formal dress. Strapless and Grecian in design, the column of platinum silk was actually quite comfortable. A Christmas gift from her mother, the dress made the most of her height and her pale skin. Instead of washing her out, the color was surprisingly flattering.

Regrettably, because of her painful leg, she would have to forgo her favorite, sparkly three-inch heels. Silver ballet flats would have to do. In the meantime, she would practice not tripping since the skirt was bound to brush the floor.

Mia had insisted on sending a car to pick up Emma at her apartment. Though Emma thought it a wasteful luxury, she had to admit that *not* having to drive was a relief.

The hours of the afternoon crept by. The cleaning lady came and went, leaving the small rooms spotless. Afterward, Emma took a bath in the old-fashioned clawfooted tub, leaning her head back and closing her eyes as she escaped to a sweeter, less volatile time in her life…

Aidan met her at the library, his hushed greeting drawing disapproving stares. Perhaps because he dragged her against him and gave her an enthusiastic kiss. He was always doing that. The uninhibited American and the repressed Englishwoman.

"Did you get your paper turned in?" she asked, loving the way his eyes ate her up. Aidan made her feel like the world's sexiest woman. It was heady stuff for a girl who had spent much of her youth as a wallflower. Crooked teeth, a slight stammer and paralyzing shyness had made boarding school a nightmare. At home, things were not much better. The few village children who were her age were either intimidated by her title or openly

sullen, resenting the money that made her life easy in their estimation.

Aidan stroked her hair, his eyes lit with humor and lust. "My paper on the wives of Henry the Eighth? Yes. Barely. All I could think about was getting you naked again."

They had been lovers for a week. Seven glorious days that had changed her life. "Aidan," she said urgently. "Hush. I don't want to get tossed out of here."

"Won't dear old Daddy take care of any demerits?"

"Don't joke about that," she said, shivering as if a ghost had walked over her grave. "He would kill me if he knew that I—"

"Let your virginal self be ravaged?"

Her grin was reluctant. "You are such a scoundrel."

He slapped a hand over his heart. "Me? You must have me confused with someone else. I'm the man who loves you, body and soul..."

From the living room, she heard the chiming of the hour on her mantel clock. It was five-thirty already. Her pumpkin coach would be arriving in little more than an hour.

Climbing out of the tub, she dried herself with a thick Turkish towel and sat in front of the mirror to twist her hair into a complicated style befitting the dress. When that was done, she applied makeup with a light hand. A bit of blush, a hint of glittery powder at her cleavage. Mascara to darken her too-pale lashes, and finally, a spritz of her favorite perfume and a quick slick of lip gloss.

Hobbling into the bedroom at a much slower pace than usual, she dragged open her lingerie drawer and selected a matching set of silk undies in pale celery green. Since it was too cold and damp to go bare legged, she added a lacy garter belt and cobweb-thin stockings with a naughty seam up the back.

She might be dateless tonight, but that was no reason to let her spirits drag. It was Christmas, damn it. And she intended to squeeze every last bit of ho-ho-ho cheer out of the occasion. Aidan and his judgmental attitude could take a hike to the North Pole and stay there for all she cared.

It was becoming increasingly clear that her move to Silver Glen might have been ill-advised, at least when it came to Aidan. He didn't want to hear anything she had to say. But fortunately, he would be gone soon—back to the big city where he could wine and dine every woman in Manhattan if he wanted to.

Emma had finally found a place where she felt at home. After so many years in Boston, she was out of step with her English roots. And city living in Massachusetts really hadn't suited her, despite enjoying her job. She was really a small-town girl when all was said and done.

Here, in Silver Glen, she had a future. Her business was off to a good start. She had the opportunity to meet new people. Even if Aidan never gave her a chance to make things right between them, his charming hometown offered a cozy place to create her nest.

At twenty 'til seven, she realized that since her accident she had never actually tried negotiating the steps to the street. Slipping into her winter dress coat and adding a filmy scarf that would serve as a shawl later, she grabbed her purse, locked the apartment door and slowly made her way downstairs.

Apparently, she had taken her pre-accident fitness for granted, bounding up and down the steep staircase several times a day. Tonight, by the time she made it to street level, her leg throbbed and she trembled. Fortunately, the uniformed driver was early and immediately opened the car door when he saw her appear.

Emma sank into the comfortable backseat and folded her hands in her lap, her heart racing. Like Cinderella being escorted to the ball, she wondered what lay ahead. No Prince Charming, that's for sure. More likely a grumpy beast. Aidan had made his feelings clear.

Pulling onto the large flagstone apron that led to sweeping steps accessing the doors of the Silver Beeches Lodge, the driver halted the car and jumped out to come around and open Emma's door. The scene that awaited her was magnificent. Two huge Fraser firs, adorned with white lights and silvery stars, flanked the hotel's entrance. On the porch, a dozen more trees, each decked out as one of the twelve days of Christmas, cast a glow against the night sky.

Though the rain had stopped, the air was misty and cold, much too chilly to linger outside. Stepping into the lobby was equally impressive. Here, a Victorian holiday theme had overtaken the large public area. On a huge round table that normally supported a lavish flower arrangement in an ornate urn, poinsettias had been stacked in tiers to form the shape of a crimson-and-green tree.

Much of the traditional décor reminded Emma of her childhood during the month of December. All she needed was a mince pie and some plum pudding and she would feel right at home.

A formal doorman took her coat and greeted her, directing her toward the ballroom at the rear of the main floor. Emma hesitated in the doorway, feeling abashed at the swirl of light and color and conversation. Gold and green festoons draped the room along the ceiling. Bunches of real mistletoe hung from curling red ropes.

Twined in the quartet of chandeliers were narrow red-and-green-plaid ribbons.

Everywhere, the air carried the scent from great boughs of evergreens that adorned the massive fireplaces on either end of the room. Before Emma could turn tail and run, Mia spotted her and hurried across the floor, her smile infectious. "I'm so glad you're here," she said. "Come let me introduce you to some of our friends."

Dylan and Mia were well liked. Emma lost count of the townspeople she met. Fortunately, there were no seats at the family tables, so Emma courted invisibility by seating herself with a couple of business owners she had met soon after she'd moved in to her storefront.

Maeve had planned the evening to the last detail. First was a sumptuous four-course dinner, beginning with cranberry salad, then butternut squash soup, and finally, the entrée consisting of squab, asparagus with Hollandaise sauce, twice-baked potatoes and yeast rolls. The china, crystal, silver and napkins were impeccable.

By the time the sweet carts rolled out, Emma was stuffed, but not so much that she couldn't enjoy a piece of pecan pie.

Her tablemates were chatty and kind, including Emma in their conversations. She found herself smiling for no particular reason except that she was happy to be there.

As the dessert course wrapped up, Dylan stood and, on behalf of Mia and himself, thanked the crowd for their gift donations. He named a total that made Emma blink. Not that she wasn't accustomed to moving in social circles where fundraising dinners were de rigueur, but many of the Kavanagh party attendees seemed like ordinary people.

After Dylan's brief speech, several people toasted the bride-and-groom-to-be, and then it was time for dancing.

A small orchestra set up shop in one corner of the room. The lights dimmed. Music filled the air. Holiday songs and romantic ballads and even a smattering of classical pieces coaxed brave couples onto the floor in the center of the room.

Emma watched wistfully. She should probably slip out. This was not the time to be without a date.

Before she could make her excuses to her tablemates and head unobtrusively to the exit, Mia appeared unexpectedly with Aidan in tow. "Emma…" Her smile was conspiratorial. "I told my future brother-in-law you were feeling much better. I know you met under odd circumstances, but we should celebrate, don't you think? You could have been badly hurt. And since neither of you has a date tonight…"

One look at Aidan's face told Emma this was not his idea. "I'm sure Aidan has lots of people he wants to chat with since he lives out of town. I'll just sit and listen to the music." She tried to back out gracefully, but though Mia was quiet by nature, she was a woman of strong opinions.

Mia tugged Emma to her feet. "Don't be silly. Aidan *wants* to dance, don't you?" She looked up at her fiancé's brother with a cajoling smile.

Aidan nodded stiffly. "Of course. If Emma's up to it."

He was giving her an out…perhaps giving *both* of them an out. Perversely, his patent reluctance made her want to irritate him. "I'd love to dance," she said, draping her scarf across the back of her chair. The room was plenty warm. With two large-scale fires blazing and the body heat from a hundred guests, she was definitely not going to get a chill.

Mia, her job done, waved a hand and went to reclaim Dylan for the next dance. Emma and Aidan stood in a small cocoon of awkward silence. He wore a tux, as did most of the men in the room. Only in Aidan's case, the formal attire fit him so comfortably and so well, he seemed in his element. A man who, no doubt, had a closet full of such clothes back in New York.

He was bigger than the boy she remembered. His shoulders—barely contained by the expensive fabric of his jacket—were broad, his belly flat. When he took her hand and pulled her into a traditional embrace, she felt a little giddy.

Was it wrong to be glad that Mia was bossy and that Aidan was too much of a gentleman to make a scene? Emma bit her lip, looking anywhere but at his face. One of his hands, fingers splayed, rested against the back of her gown just below the place where bare skin met soft fabric.

She had intended to make light conversation, but her throat dried up. A wave of nostalgia and sexual yearning swept over her with such force that she stumbled once. Aidan righted her effortlessly, his strong legs moving them with ease across the crowded dance floor.

When Aidan spoke, she actually jumped.

"Relax," he said, his tone frustrated. "I'm not going to out you to the room. No one needs to know our dirty secrets."

Her spine locked straight. "We don't have any dirty secrets," she said, enunciating carefully.

"Then why haven't you told my family who you really are?"

Finally, she allowed her gaze to meet his. If she had expected to see tumultuous emotion, she was way off base. His face was a pleasant mask, only a tic in his cheek betraying any hint of agitation. "Who am I?" she asked pointedly. "An old girlfriend? That hardly seems worth mentioning. We were little more than children playing at being grown-ups."

Finally, she stirred the sleeping dragon. Fire shot from his eyes, searing her nerves and making her tremble. "Don't you dare," he said, the words forced from between clenched teeth. "It may have been a long time ago, but I won't let you rewrite history so you can whitewash the truth."

"The truth?" She stared up at him, confused and upset. "I don't know what you mean."

"You screwed me over, Emma. Though I must admit that your prissy English manners almost made it seem like a privilege. I was a young fool. But I learned my lesson. When I told you I didn't want to talk about the past, I meant it. But apparently, it's not so easy to overlook."

"I didn't ask you to dance with me," she said, the words bitter in her mouth.

"You didn't put up much of a fight, either."

To any onlookers, it must have appeared that Aidan and Emma were conversing politely in the midst of a dance.

Suddenly, she couldn't bear to have him touching her. Not when she knew how much he despised her.

"I will *not* cause a scene and ruin Mia's party." Her tone was soft but vehement. "But I am leaving this dance floor—now."

"Not without me." The fake smile he plastered on his face was in direct counterpoint to the unrelenting grip of his fingers around her wrist as he walked casually away from the dancers, pulling Emma in his wake.

If she struggled, everyone would see.

She waited until they reached the relative privacy of the hallway until trying to jerk free. "Let go of me, damn it."

But Aidan wasn't done. He stared down at her, a slash of red on each of his cheekbones. The glitter in his eyes could have been anger—or something far more volatile.

"We're going upstairs," he said. "And we're going to hash out a few things.

"My scarf and purse are at the table."

"I'll call and ask them to hold your things at the front desk."

"Oh, good," she said, glaring at him. "At least someone will know I've gone missing."

Seven

Aidan knew the moment they stepped into the elevator that he had made a strategic mistake. The mirrored walls reflected Emma's cool, English beauty no matter where he turned his gaze. The swanlike grace of her neck. The perfect features…even the vulnerable spot at her nape that he had unfortunately fantasized about all evening.

She carried herself with the poise of a Grecian goddess who might have worn such a dress once upon a time. The only flaw he could see was the slight limp caused by the injury to her leg. She had used makeup to cover the stitches near her ear. They were barely noticeable.

From the first moment he saw her tonight with her hair intricately woven around her head, he had wanted nothing more than to remove each pin, one by one, and watch all that golden silk tumble down around her bare shoulders.

They reached his floor in a matter of seconds. Emma made no move to elude him. Perhaps she knew they had been heading for this moment all along.

When he opened the door of his suite and ushered her inside, she glanced around curiously but did not comment. The accommodations were luxurious, but for a woman of Emma's background, the antique furnishings and Oriental rugs were old hat.

"Would you like a drink?" he asked.

She perched on the edge of a chair, her hands folded in her lap. "Whiskey. Neat."

He raised an eyebrow. The girl he had known rarely drank anything stronger than wine. Perhaps she was more nervous that he realized. It was petty of him to be glad. But he was.

When he handed her the heavy crystal tumbler, she eyed him over the rim, tossed back her head and swallowed the shot in one gulp. She might be nervous, but she was defiant as hell.

Taking a sip of his own drink, he rested a hip against the arm of the sofa, too antsy to sit down.

Emma finally relaxed enough to lean back in her chair. Kicking off her small shoes, she curled her legs beneath her. For a moment he caught a glimpse of slim ankles and berry-painted toes before she twitched her skirt to cover the view.

"I find myself at a loss," he said. "I know you're up to something, but since my sister and my mother have taken you to their bosom, I can hardly toss you out on your ear."

"I live here now," she said, her gaze daring him to disagree.

"And why is that?"

"You didn't want any explanations," she reminded him, the words tart.

"Perhaps I was too hasty." He offered the conciliatory olive branch, but Emma stomped on it.

"The information window is closed." Her ironic smile and visible satisfaction at thwarting him made his temper spark, but he was determined to keep the upper hand.

"What if we agree to an exchange? One piece of info for another."

"I don't need to know anything about you. I don't care."

If the way her breasts heaved was any indication—threatening their containment—she cared far more than she was letting on.

He poured her another drink. "I forgot to ask if you were still taking pain pills."

She took the second shot and treated it like the first. Though her face turned red and her eyes watered, she never wavered. "Of course not. I'm not stupid."

"I never said you were. Everyone at Oxford was quick to point out to me that you were one of the smartest women on campus."

"Not too smart, apparently."

"What does that mean?"

"Oh, never mind." She seemed crestfallen suddenly, her lower lip trembling, her expression lost.

"I own a very lavish penthouse apartment in the heart of New York City. I deal in high-end real estate."

"Believe me, Aidan. That's not exactly news. Your mother has been singing your praises in great detail. She misses you."

"I'm here now."

"Yes, you are."

"Look at me."

He strode to where she sat, pulled her to her feet, and settled them both on the sofa. Finishing his own drink, he placed his glass on the coffee table. "Actually, there's only one thing I really need to know."

She half turned to face him, her wide-eyed gaze curious. The platinum silk molded to her body with mesmerizing results. "What's that?"

"I'll show you." Capturing her mouth beneath his, he kissed her slowly, allowing her every opportunity to resist. Nowhere did their bodies touch except for the breathless press of lips on lips.

Her scent was familiar—sweet English roses with a hint of dewy spring. He'd been down this road a hundred times...heard the same angel choirs...seen the land of milk and honey.

His heart slugged in his chest, struggling to keep up with the need for oxygen. His circulatory system was taxed to the limit, as if his blood had become thick molasses.

In his head he heard the raucous sound submarines make when diving. Something was pulling him under. Something dangerous.

Emma made no move to put her hands on him. He was the one to crack first. Helpless, desperate, he slid both hands alongside her neck and angled her chin with his thumbs.

The room was silent except for their harsh breathing. He felt as if he were floating on the ceiling, watching himself fall through the same rabbit hole. At one time, Emma's kisses had been the magic elixir that made his days in England as bright and sweet as a dream.

He was losing control. His brain knew it. His body fought the truth. Shuddering with a desire that shredded his resolve, he used one hand to tug at the bodice of her dress. The thin fabric yielded easily, as did the filmy lace of her bra. In moments his fingertips caressed the puckered tip of one breast, then the other.

Emma groaned. "Aidan..." The word was barely a whisper.

He leaned over her warm, curvy body stretched out on the sofa. Abandoning her lips with no small amount of regret, he moved lower to kiss her more intimately, using his teeth to scrape furled nipples.

So lost was he in the feast that was her body, it took several long seconds for him to recognize the moment when she rebelled. Small hands beat at his shoulders. "No more, Aidan. No more."

Groggy with shock and confusion, he sat up, moving away from her with haste. In her face he saw what they had done. In her eyes he saw the woman he had loved more than was sane.

"God help me," he muttered, unable to look away as Emma tugged her dress into place. Several strands of her hair had come loose to dangle onto her shoulders. She looked rumpled and well loved.

She sat up as well, her complexion paler than the night he'd brought her home from the hospital.

Rage and fear consumed him. He stared at her in silence, his chest roiling with emotions to which he dared not give a name. Self-preservation kicked in. He wiped his mouth with the back of his hand, removing traces of lip color. "Amazing," he said, his heart as cold as his hands. "How can you look like a princess, kiss like a siren and have the duplicitous heart of a cheat and a liar?"

Emma blinked. He saw the moment she processed his deliberate insult. Dark color flooded her face. She smacked him hard with an open palm. The sound echoed. "How dare you," she cried, as moisture brightened her eyes. "You don't even know me. Apparently you never did."

He shrugged, insolent and furious, as much at himself as at her. "I know enough. I won't be wrapped around your finger again, Lady Emma. I learned my lesson."

She lifted her chin, as though daring the teardrops to fall. "You're a miserable, hardened, shallow man. You've let your prejudices and your grudges and your righteous indignation blind you. I can't believe I ever thought I was in love with you."

"But you never really were. It was all a charade.

Though for the life of me I can't understand why you bothered. Was having a fling with an American something on your bucket list? Or did you simply want to defy your father and prove your independence?"

Emma stared at him, her lips pressed together in a thin line. If there were a prize for dignity, she would win it every time. He *knew* she was in the wrong, and she knew it as well. Yet somehow, she managed to look like the injured innocent. Making him the villain.

"I'm going home," she said, the words flat. "You've made your point. Do us both a favor and keep your distance."

She jumped to her feet abruptly, obviously intending to reach for her shoes. But she tripped on the hem of her dress and slammed into the coffee table. Her cry of pain made him wince. Blood colored the skirt of her dress, no doubt from the stitches on her leg.

"Good Lord," he said. "What have you done to yourself?"

Not waiting for permission, he scooped her up and took her to his bedroom. Flipping back the covers to protect the expensive duvet, he set her down and unceremoniously lifted her dress.

"Don't touch me." She batted his hands away. The tears she had held at bay earlier fell now. Silent wet tracks that dripped onto her bosom.

"Settle down," he muttered. "Let me see what you've done." He took her ankle in his hand and bent to get a closer look. The bones beneath her skin seemed impossibly fragile. Touching her hastened his own defeat. But he had no defense. The feel of her skin beneath rough fingertips did something terrible to his resolve not to get sucked in again. He would have to keep up his guard.

He didn't care about her. Of course he didn't. It had

been a decade. Only his libido had any interest in pursuing this inconveniently persistent attraction. Emma Braithwaite was a stunning woman. It was normal for him, or any man, to react to her sexuality. In fact, if he *weren't* affected by her allure, he would be worried.

The carefully worded but unspoken argument did little to settle the churning in his stomach.

The wound on her leg had been healing nicely, but the blow to her shin evidently had landed in exactly the wrong place. One end of the reddened seam had pulled apart maybe an eighth of an inch and was bleeding profusely. "We need to go back to the emergency room," he said.

"No. I don't want to. I have butterfly bandages at home. That will take care of it."

She tried to pull her skirt down, but he held the cloth firmly. Her bare thighs were slim and supple. *Damn it...* He cleared his throat. "You don't want a nasty scar."

"The worst scars are the ones you can't see."

Her eyes met his. Their gazes clung. Something hovered in the air. Memory. Regret.

He almost kissed her again. The urge was overpowering, his need vital and pressing. "Don't move," he said. "I have some Band-Aids in my shaving kit. That will cover it until you get home."

His miscalculation cost him. Perhaps he had misunderstood the import of their kiss, because he had been in the bathroom no longer than thirty seconds when he heard the door to his room slam shut. Rushing out to stop her, he saw the empty bed. The bed that already figured prominently in his dreams at night—only in the dreams, he was not alone...

Emma's skin glowed like pearls in the shaft of moonlight that fell through her window. The bed was narrow, the sheets unexceptional. For a student apartment, the two-room space was above average. Aidan barely noticed his surroundings. How could he with a naked Emma on her back waiting to love him?

Ripping off the last of his clothes and donning a condom, he gave her a quick grin. "Scoot over. There's no place for me."

She bent one knee, placing her foot flat against the mattress. The sight of her feminine secrets made his hands shake.

"I suppose you'll have to climb on top," she said, her smile droll and mischievous.

The sex was still new. He felt like a fumbling peasant in the presence of royalty. Not that Emma gave herself airs. But because she was so damned perfect. He was hard and ready. But still he waited.

Emma seemed to read his mind. "I won't break," she said softly. "I love it that you want me so much. It's the same for me."

It couldn't be. No one could feel what he felt in that moment...

He sat on the edge of the bed and put his head in his hands, his elbows on his knees. How ironic that he had been so worried about recollections of Danielle during the holidays, when in fact, the worst memories of all were the ones about him and Emma that had blindsided him.

The urge to jump in his car almost won. He could be back in New York by morning if he managed to stay awake. Emma would understand, once and for all, that her ploy hadn't worked...whatever it was.

But his mother would never forgive him. And he wouldn't forgive himself. It would be unbearably selfish to let his problems ruin Dylan and Mia's wedding day. Equally as bad would be abandoning his family at Christmas. They were all so wretchedly glad to see him. As if he were the prodigal son returning after a long absence.

He came home to Silver Glen all the time, damn it.

But not in December. And now he was paying the price.

Since he had no choice in the matter, he would have to take Emma's suggestion and stay as far away as possible. Otherwise, he couldn't trust himself not to beg. That was the bitterest pill of all to swallow. Despite the fact that she had humiliated and betrayed him, given half a chance, he would willingly forget the past for one more night in her bed.

It was laughable now to think he had taught himself not to feel. Of course he felt. He felt it all. Everything from the purifying blaze of well-founded anger to the crazed urge to let his lust dictate the course of the next ten days.

The choice was his. All he had to do was let Emma speak her piece. Presumably, she had some explanation for lying to him. He could pretend to believe her and they could wallow in erotic excess until it was time for him to go home to New York. The hunger that turned him inside out would be appeased.

The idea had a certain wicked appeal. But like making a deal with the devil, if he gave in to temptation, his soul would never be his own again. If he bedded her, skin-to-skin, nothing between them but the air they breathed, he might decide he could live with the past.

When whatever game she was playing ended, there was the reality that she would lie to him again. Women didn't change. He hadn't been enough for her once before and she had crushed him with her betrayal.

Could he do it for the sex? Could he draw a line in the sand and take only what he wanted? He'd sealed off his heart long ago. No woman since Emma had managed to tempt him. Except for his family, he cared about no one. He was a hollow man.

Pain came with relationships. His father had abandoned him by putting his obsessions ahead of his family. Danielle had abandoned him by dying. But in Emma's case, Aidan had been the one to leave. As soon as he learned the truth, he didn't hang around to be kicked in the teeth again. Even so, that pain had been the worst of all.

Eight

Emma cleaned blood off her leg and pondered all the ways she could murder Aidan Kavanagh in his sleep. He was infuriating and stubborn and his masculine arrogance made her want to hurl things at his head.

He still felt something for her. Even if it was only lust. But no way in heck was she going to tumble into bed with him when he thought so little of her. Perhaps she should have insisted on clearing the air immediately when he first recognized her. After all, the reason she'd come to Silver Glen, in part, was to make amends for the way she'd handled things in the past. She had hurt both Aidan *and* herself, though he bore some responsibility as well.

Maybe her stubborn pride was as bad as his, because she didn't want to make her apologies to a man who said he didn't care enough to hear what she had to say. There were a lot of things they could talk about. Important things. In her personal version of a twelve-step program, making amends was high up on the list. But it was hard to do that when the person you injured wouldn't let you do what you needed to do.

It was probably just as well. Look at what happened tonight. It was a really bad idea for the two of them to relive their college infatuation. Sex would introduce a whole extra layer of entanglement, because Aidan's family had no idea that Emma and Aidan shared a past.

Still, when she thought about his kiss, it was difficult not to imagine what would have come next. Feeling his hands on her body had kindled a fire, a yearning to experience his possession one more time. No man in the last ten years had made her feel a fraction of what Aidan could, not that many had tried.

Americans attributed her standoffishness to British reserve. But it wasn't that. Not really. She wasn't shy. She had simply learned to protect herself. Meeting Aidan at Oxford was a chance encounter. She'd been freer back then, more apt to take a chance on love.

Now, she was mostly happy on her own. Men complicated life. She had girlfriends back in Boston. And here in Silver Glen, she was already building a circle of support. She wanted to make things right with Aidan. But if that never happened, at least she had found a place to call home.

She glanced at the clock on the wall, realizing that the hour was really not that late. Even so, she was beat. Her first outing since her accident had required more energy than she realized. Suddenly, the idea of curling up in bed for an early night was impossible to resist.

After brewing a cup of herbal tea, she set it on her dresser while she changed into a comfy flannel nightgown. Then, moving the tea to the bedside table, she sat down on the mattress, plumped the pillows behind her back and picked up the novel she was in the midst of reading. She managed to finish her tea, but just barely. After her eyelids drifted shut for the third time, she gave up, climbed under the covers and turned out the light.

* * *

Sometime later, an insistent noise woke her. In the dark, she listened carefully, her heartbeat syncopated. It took only a moment to process that the sound she heard was the street-level buzzer. It rang upstairs whenever she had a visitor.

Leaning up on one elbow, she hit the button on her phone and gazed at the time blearily. Good grief.

Since the person at the other end of the buzzer didn't appear to be dissuaded by her lack of response, she got up, shoved her feet into slippers and reached for her fleecy robe. Her wound was still tender, but the Band-Aid had stopped the bleeding.

In the living room, she pushed aside the sheers and looked down at the street. There were no cars in sight except for her neighbor's familiar sedan. But even from this angle she could see the figure of a man.

As if he could feel her watching him, he stepped back, looked toward her window and made a familiar let-me-in motion.

Clearly, she should ignore him. He would go away soon.

Even as she lectured herself, her feet carried her down the steep stairs. Her hand on the doorknob, she called out, "Who is it?"

With only a couple of inches of wood separating them, she could hear the response distinctly. "You know who it is. Open the door, Emma."

Her toes curled inside her slippers. "Why?"

"Do you really want the whole town to know our business?" he muttered.

The man had a point. She jerked open the door and stared at him. He was bareheaded despite the fact that it was frigid outside. "Do you have any idea what time it is?" she asked, trying to sound irritated instead of excited. There was only one reason a man came calling at this hour. The intensity of his shadowy gaze made her pulse jump and dance.

"No. I don't. But I'm freezing out here. May I please come in?"

She stepped back to allow the door to close, and suddenly the two of them were practically mashed together in the handkerchief-sized space. "Where is your car, Aidan?"

He shrugged, his clothes smelling like the outdoors. It was a nice fragrance, a combination of cold air and evergreen. "I walked," he said bluntly. "We'd had a few drinks, if you remember."

"That's at least five miles." She gaped, unable to comprehend such a crazy thing in the middle of the night.

"Why do you think it took me so long to get here?"

"Oh, for goodness' sakes. Come on up. I'll make you a hot drink. Can you deal with coffee at this hour?"

He followed on her heels. "I'll take some of your famous herbal tea."

In the kitchen, he took off his wool overcoat and tossed it over a chair. The light was too bright. She felt exposed, though she was covered from head to toe. His sharp gaze took in her decidedly unseductive attire. Though his lips twitched, he made no comment.

He still wore his tux pants and white shirt, but he'd left his jacket behind. The shirt was unbuttoned partway down his chest. A partial night's beard shadowed his firm jaw. He looked sexy and dangerous, like a man who was about to throw caution to the wind.

What did it say about her that his rakish air stirred her? That his undiluted masculinity was both mesmerizing and exciting?

He sat down in one of her spindly wooden chairs, his weight making the joints creak. For the first time she recognized his fatigue. Was it because of the hour or because of his nighttime prowl or because he had been wrestling with himself? The third option was one she understood all too well. Why else had she opened her door?

Without speaking, she handed him a cup of tea and poured one for herself. Instead of joining him at the table, she leaned against the fridge, keeping a safe distance between them.

"Why are you here, Aidan?"

The satirical look he gave her questioned her intelligence. "Don't be coy."

She shrugged. "Does this mean you're ready to listen to my explanations?"

"I told you before. I don't want to hear anything about the past or why you're here in Silver Glen."

"What else is there?"

He stood abruptly and plucked the china cup out of her hand. "This."

Dragging her flush against his big frame, he dove in for a hard, punishing kiss, one arm tight across her back. His lips moved on hers with confidence...as if he remembered in exquisite detail exactly what she liked.

The old Aidan had never been this sure of himself. But darned if she didn't like it. Without shoes, she was at a distinct disadvantage, though. She stood on her tiptoes, straining to align her mouth with his. Everything about him was warm and wonderful. Despite his gruff refusal to let her plead for absolution, there was tenderness in his kiss.

She shivered, even though in Aidan's embrace she was perfectly warm. Too warm, maybe. She felt dizzy. As if all the air had been sucked out of the room.

"I want you, Emma," he muttered. "Tell me you want me, too."

It was a hard thing to deny when her arms were twined around his neck in a stranglehold. "Yes," she said. "I do, but—"

He put his hand over her mouth, stilling her words. "No buts," he said firmly. He paused for a moment, the look on his face impossible to decipher. "There's only one question I need answered." His Adam's apple bobbed as he swallowed. "Are you married?"

Shock immobilized her. She twisted out of his embrace, staring at him wide-eyed. "No. *No.*" She answered more forcefully the second time.

"Good." He picked up her left hand and lifted it to his lips. "Then, Lady Emma Braithwaite, will you do me the honor of taking me to your bed?" His droll smile was at odds with the intensity of his gaze. A tiny muscle ticked in his granite jaw as though her answer was far more important than he was letting on.

Emma had come to that moment in life when plans had gone awry and the road ahead was no longer clear. "Do you hate me?" she asked bluntly. "For what happened?"

Aidan was unable to hide his wince. "Does it look like I hate you? I'm practically eating out of your hand, damn it."

It wasn't really an answer to her question. "Please, Aidan. Tell me the truth."

His broad shoulders lifted and fell. Full, masculine lips twisted. "No. I don't hate you." He paced the confines of her small kitchen. "There was a time when I *wanted* to hate you, but no more. Life is short. I'll be leaving soon. I think we can chalk up tonight to what-might-have-been. It's Christmas. I'm feeling an odd, sentimental need to be somebody else tonight. Somebody that I used to know. A boy, not quite a man. An idealistic, heart-on-his-sleeve kid. Too naïve to be let loose in the wild."

For the first time, she understood that he was telling her the God's honest truth.

"I loved that boy," she whispered. "He was amazing and kind and perfect in every way."

"He was a fool." The blunt exclamation held a trace of bitterness and anger, despite his professed lack of enmity.

"I won't let you say that." Her tone was firm. Though Aidan Kavanagh was a mature, successful man, she saw in painful clarity the many ways she had damaged him. "If you don't want to rehash the past, then so be it. We'll make tonight all about the present. Come to bed with me."

He paled beneath his tan. "No regrets when the cold light of day dawns, Emma. From either of us. I need your promise. I won't be accused of taking advantage of you."

Crossing her fingers left and right over her heart, she lifted her chin and eyed him steadily, even though her chest jumped and wiggled with fizzy shards of happiness. "No regrets."

Quietly, he switched off the kitchen light and followed her to her bedroom. The sheets and comforter were tumbled where she had leapt up quickly to answer the door. Stopping beside the bed, she battled a sudden attack of shyness.

Aidan had no such problem. He removed her robe with gentle motions, and then touched the button at her collarbone, unfastening it along with three more. "Lift your arms," he commanded.

When she obeyed, he pulled the gown over her head. She wore not a stitch beneath it. He had her naked in less than five seconds.

The look on his face was gratifying. He brushed his thumb over her navel. Gooseflesh broke out all over her body.

"You're cold," he said.

She shook her head slowly. "Not cold. Just ready."

When he lifted her into his arms, she was confused. They were both at the bed already. But as she rested her cheek against his chest and looked up at him, her heart twisted. For a split second, she saw the young man who had loved her with such reckless generosity and passion.

He stared down at her for long seconds. She could almost feel his turmoil. "No one needs to know about this," he said.

Though the words hurt, she nodded. "I understand."

"Birth control?" His communication had been reduced to simple phrases, as though he barely retained the capacity to speak.

"I'm on the pill. And no health problems to worry about."

"Nor I." He shook his head as if to clear it. "I'm not sure I can wait any longer."

She cupped his cheek with her hand. "Why would you? We're both on the same page tonight, Aidan. Make love to me."

Hesitating, he stared at her with stormy eyes. "This is sex. No more, no less."

Not love. Message received.

"Whatever you want to call it is fine by me. Now if you'll excuse me, I need to freshen up."

Fleeing to the bathroom, she leaned her hands on the counter and stared into the mirror. Her cheeks were flushed, her pupils dilated. Was she making a monumental mistake? Was it wrong to share her bed with Aidan when there were so many things left unsaid?

A slight noise in the bedroom reminded her that there was no time for dithering. Either she wanted him, or she didn't. When you put it that way, there was only one clear answer.

She took two minutes to prepare. Then she opened the door, squared her bare shoulders and returned to the bedroom.

Nine

Aidan couldn't believe this was happening. How many times over the years had he imagined this very scenario? Or dreamed it, vividly erotic in his head?

As he stripped off his pants and boxers, socks and shoes, he was painfully aware that he had been hard for the better part of the evening. Dancing with Emma was a particularly wicked kind of torture. Now, naked and lovely, she stared at him, her nervousness impossible to hide. He wanted to reassure her, but in truth, he had no reassurances to give. What they were about to do was either self-destructive, or at the very least unwise. Even knowing that, he couldn't work up any enthusiasm for the idea of being sensible.

"You're beautiful," he said. It seemed a trite thing to mention. Surely the men in her life had been telling her as much since she was an innocent sweet sixteen.

Her hands twisted at her waist as though she wanted to cover herself. She was clean-shaven between her legs except for a tiny strip of blond fluff that proved her hair color was natural. Her legs were long and shapely, her waist narrow, her breasts high and firm.

If he were strictly impartial, he might note that her forehead was too high for classic beauty…and her nose a tad too sharp. But those minor flaws were balanced out by the heart-shaped face, full pink lips and eyes the color of an October sky.

He took one of her hands in his, finding it icy. Chafing it carefully, he cocked his head toward the pile of covers. "I think in December the preliminaries should probably be carried out in bed. I don't want you to catch pneumonia."

"This feels awkward," she said with blunt honesty and a crooked smile of apology.

He nodded. "It will get better."

They moved, one at a time, into the relative warmth of the bed. The sheets seemed chilled, but heated rapidly.

Emma reclined on her side facing him, head propped on a feather pillow. She watched him with fascination and reserve. "You must have lots of experience," she said, the words hinting at dissatisfaction.

He mirrored her position, though he propped his head on his hand. "I doubt we want to compare notes on our sexual histories. Do we?"

"No. I suppose not."

In her pose and in her gaze he saw the same thing that had drawn him to her when he was at university. There was no other way to describe it than *goodness*. It radiated from her. No woman he'd ever met appeared to be so unsullied, so open and warm.

Yet, he knew for a fact that it was only a facade. Emma had a capacity for deception, as indeed did most humans. Aidan made no assumptions about her. He had not listened to malicious lies. He'd gone straight to the source, had asked Emma for the truth. Even now, recalling that moment stabbed his heart with disillusionment.

Shaking off the unpleasant memory, he concentrated on the woman who was so close, her breath mingling with his. Reaching out, he stroked her hair, sifting the strands through his fingertips. "We were so young," he said. "But I thought you were the most exquisite thing I had ever seen."

"And you were brash and handsome and charmingly affable. A young Hugh Grant. Except with that adorable American accent."

Aidan chuckled. "Perhaps it's true that opposites attract. I was mortifyingly intimidated by your pedigree and your finishing school manners." He moved a fingertip lazily from her cheek to her collarbone to her cleavage. Emma's sharp intake of breath told him that the simple touch affected her as strongly as it did him.

Gently, he pressed her shoulder, urging her onto her back. As he shifted positions to lean over her on one elbow, he mapped her body with his palm. Plump, curvy breasts. Smooth rib cage. Almost concave belly. And then—the mother lode.

Keeping his gaze fixed on hers, he traced the folds of her sex with gentle persuasion. Her legs moved restlessly, her thighs widening in unspoken invitation. It would be so easy to pounce and take. But since his plan was to allow himself only a single night of delirium, he had to go slowly. Make it last. Wring every drop of pleasure from the hushed minutes when he had her to himself.

Emma's hands roved over his scalp, her fingers sweeping across his forehead, stroking his neck, playing with his ears. It was embarrassing that such chaste touches made him rigid with need. His erection was full and hard and throbbing with eagerness.

Do it. Take her. Now.

Every masculine impulse leaned toward plunder. Only the mitigating tenderness of their past reined him in.

Emma exhaled in a shuddering sigh. "When you touch me, I melt inside. It was always that way, Aidan."

Perhaps that much was the truth. He would never really know. But she couldn't fake her body's response at the moment. The warm, soft welcome at her center was slick and moist and scented with her need.

He had intended to tease them both with long minutes of foreplay. But why? He couldn't want her more. No hunger could be as gut-wrenching. He was primed and ready.

Moving over her on shaking arms, he positioned the head of his sex at her entrance and pushed with a groan that betrayed his need. Her excitement eased his passage, taking him to the hilt with oxygen-stealing speed. *Holy hell.* Either his memories were faulty or she had slipped some kind of aphrodisiac into his tea.

"Damn, Emma."

She arched her back, taking him deeper still. Her legs wrapped around his waist, her heels locking in the small of his back. "Don't stop," she begged, the words ragged.

Cursing and laughing, he moved in her with what little control he had left. "Not a problem."

To say they were good together was like saying the horizon was infinite. He'd had plenty of sex in his adult life. But whatever happened when he joined his body with Emma's defied description.

A sappy English poet might talk about roses and hearts afire and the purity of true love. Aidan took a more visceral approach. When he screwed Emma, his body went berserk. Fireworks, explosions, searing heat…incandescent pleasure.

And all that was before he climaxed.

He buried his hot face in her neck. "Once won't be enough."

She bit the side of his neck. "I never said it would."

Feeling her teeth on him was all it took. Light flashed behind his eyelids. He pistoned his hips. In some dim corner of his brain, he tried to make sure he gave her what she needed. If her wild cries were any indication, he was succeeding.

Then he went rigid as the world went black and he lost himself in the flash fire of completion.

Emma trembled uncontrollably. Most of Aidan's weight pressed her into the bed. His breathing was harsh and uneven. She had no idea if he were awake or asleep. She was hoping for the latter, because she hadn't a clue what she was supposed to say.

Wow, Aidan. That was awesome. Let's do it again.

Or…*you rocked my world. And I'm pretty sure I never stopped loving you.*

Hysteria bubbled in her chest. She was in so much trouble. How had she blinded herself to the truth? She hadn't come to Silver Glen to find Aidan and make amends for their past…or at least not only that. She wanted to win him back.

Since the chances of that happening were about as good as the possibility of the Queen dancing naked beside the Thames, Emma had a choice to make. She could slink away quietly and go home to England—forgetting she ever knew Aidan Kavanagh—*or* she could fight for him. But the emotional barriers he had built were formidable.

Confrontation was not Emma's strong suit. Aidan didn't want to hear her version of the past. Anytime she tried to bring it up, he stonewalled her. But tonight, he had given her a powerful weapon. He had shown her clearly that at least one thing hadn't changed over the years. He and Emma were still magic between the sheets.

That had to count for something, right?

She smoothed his hair with her hand, relishing the opportunity to touch him as she wished. How different her life might have been if she'd had more gumption at twenty-one…if she hadn't been under her father's thumb…if she'd had the confidence to accept that the handsome American really loved her.

But deep in her heart, she had doubted Aidan. It shamed her to admit it. And it had taken her a long time to face the truth. One reason their relationship had ended so abruptly and with such devastating finality was that she hadn't really believed a man could want her for herself.

The preteen wallflower had grown up to be a self-conscious academic. Her degree in art history was achieved with highest honors, but no one had ever expected her to use it, least of all her family. Emma's purpose in life was to marry well and continue the Braithwaite legacy.

Perhaps to someone of Aidan's background, such a notion was antiquated. But Emma had grown up circumscribed by the expectations of her rank and position in society. Her parents adhered rigidly to the tenets of their social code. As their only child, Emma's path in life had been well defined. Even so, she'd certainly had the freedom to fall in love…as long as the man of her choice passed muster in the pages of Debrett's *Peerage & Baronetage*.

Now, holding the mature, sexy Aidan Kavanagh in her arms, she couldn't fathom that she had been so foolish. His advent into her young life had seemed like such a fairy tale, she'd lived the fantasy and refused to think about the future. Which meant that when disaster struck, she hadn't been prepared. Neither had she possessed the confidence to fight back. A mistake she bitterly regretted.

Her cowardice had hurt Aidan and destroyed their fragile, beautiful relationship. Even though she had tried her best to fix things in the aftermath, the damage had been done.

Already, she wanted him again. Hesitantly, she ran her hands down the taut planes of his back, as far as she could reach. He was a beautiful man. Naked, he seemed both more powerful and more approachable.

Moving slowly and carefully so as not to wake him, she eased him onto his back. His broad, hair-dusted chest rose and fell with his steady breathing. The flat belly, muscled thighs and surprisingly sexy feet caught her eye. But it was his quiescent sex that made her sigh with appreciation. Even at rest, it shouted his masculinity.

Men were so wonderfully different from women. In her art history classes she had studied hundreds of famous nudes—painted on canvas, chiseled in marble, sculpted in bronze. But no matter how impressive the subject, there was nothing to compare to a living, breathing man.

Resting her hand on his thigh, she bent to examine a small white scar on his right hip, probably a childhood injury. He and his brothers had been wild rascals growing up, particularly after their father died. She could only imagine how Maeve Kavanagh managed to wrangle them all into becoming upright citizens of the community.

"Em, are you window-shopping or trying to get something started?"

She sat up abruptly, shocked to the core. Apparently, Aidan was a better actor than she realized. Clearing her throat, she sat back on her heels. "How long have you been awake?"

"Long enough." He linked his hands behind his head, smiling slightly, clearly enjoying her discomfiture.

She couldn't think of an excuse that would explain her intense interest in his body. So she changed the subject.

"Sorry I woke you," she said, not quite able to meet his knowing gaze. "We should both probably get some sleep. The next three days are going to be busy."

He took her hand and tugged her down beside him. "Hush, Em. Don't be embarrassed. I want to look at you, too."

But she wasn't as blasé as he was about her nude body. Dragging the sheet to her chin, she bit her lip. "I thought you might want to go back to the hotel now."

"It's the middle of the night." He chuckled. "And I don't have a car. As far as I can tell, staying right here in your bed is a damned good plan. Do you have any objections?"

Lord, no, she thought. Why did it matter if they were sleep-deprived? It was about time some of her other physical needs took center stage for a change. She could sleep when she was old.

"You called me *Em*," she said.

His smile faded. "Don't make a big deal out of that. It slipped out. That's all. Old habits."

She hoped it was more than that. *Em* was the nickname he'd sometimes used for her when they were in college. Often he would whisper it in the midst of sex. A tender, affectionate means of address that always sounded indulgent and proprietary.

She nodded, unsure what was going to happen next. While they talked, his erection had flexed to attention again. A thing like that was hard to ignore. But the expression on Aidan's face was serious.

Touching her cheek gently, he grimaced. "Tell me why you moved from England to Silver Glen."

Her heart leapt. It was a chink in the wall, though a small one. "I didn't," she said. "I've lived in Boston for the last nine years."

"Doing what?" She had startled him, no question.

"I was an art appraiser at the Sotheby's branch there."

"Why work at all?"

"You're rich. And *you* work. We all need a reason to get up in the morning."

"Why did you leave England?"

She wanted to be a smart-ass and remind him that he wasn't interested in having information or explanations. But it would be foolish to bypass this opportunity. "I had a falling out with my father. We're both stubborn people, so neither side wanted to concede. I refused to go home for eight and a half years. My mother visited me often in Boston, but until this past spring I had not seen my father for a very long time."

"And why last spring?" He seemed genuinely curious.

The reasons for her voluntary exile to the States involved Aidan, but she didn't think he was ready to hear that. Not yet. Maybe not ever. So she told him the bare bones.

"My father was an old-school autocrat. He ruled our family with an iron fist, expecting absolute obedience. When it became clear that he and I were never going to see eye-to-eye about several very important topics, I knew I had to strike out on my own."

"Must have been scary."

"It was…but exciting, too. Even so, I missed home. When my father was diagnosed with pancreatic cancer in April, the doctors told my mother he had only weeks to live. I flew back immediately, and thankfully, I was able to reconcile with him before he left us. That experience taught me it's never too late to heal old wounds."

The personal story was about as blunt as she was prepared to be. Aidan was an intelligent man. Surely he could read between the lines. It had taken until today for Emma to acknowledge to herself that her reasons for coming to Silver Glen were more convoluted that she had been willing to admit.

She wasn't committed to any man at the moment. And unless Aidan was not the man she once knew, he was not attached either, or he would not be in bed with her. If she could convince him that what tore them apart was no longer relevant—if he would accept her apologies— then surely there was no reason they couldn't make a new start.

That was a big pile of assumptions. Built mostly on fantasy and dreams. But he was in her bed, so that was a start.

Ten

Aidan tried to find his anger and his righteous indignation, but it seemed to have disappeared along with his pants. It was difficult for a man to hold a grudge while a woman's naked body was pressed against his. He stroked Emma's hip. "Enough chitchat," he said. But he smiled to let her know he wasn't making light of her revelations.

Her hair was rumpled. Dark shadows smudged beneath her eyes spoke of exhaustion. Perhaps another man would have been content to hold her. But not Aidan. Not after waiting a decade to be with her again.

Difficulties lurked outside this room. And reality. Not to mention his vivid, painful memories of the past. For the moment, however, he was content to overlook the negatives. Probably because his brain was not in control. That function had been ceded to his baser anatomy.

He kissed her softly, one hand balanced on the pillow, his fingers tangled in her hair. "I want you again," he said. His lips moved to her eyelids, her cute nose, her perfect earlobes.

When Emma squirmed, her hand brushed his erection. Accidentally, or no? He sucked in a sharp breath. "Don't stop there." The gruff command worked. Perhaps because it sounded more like a plea. When her slender fingers closed around his firm shaft, stroking up and down, he shuddered and gasped, totally unable to hide his excitement.

Emma might have seen his reaction as proof of her power over him. But instead, her gaze was one of fascination. "I don't remember what you liked," she said quietly, as if confessing a wretched secret.

"No complaints here." He forced the words between clenched teeth. She was adorable. But then she always had been. He refused to think about any other men who might have been part of her life. He didn't want to know. If he could keep his mind on the present and nothing else, everything would be okay.

"Aidan?" She abandoned her activity and put both hands on his cheeks lightly.

He turned his face and kissed one soft palm. "What?"

Big eyes searched his as if seeking answers to questions they hadn't even spoken aloud. "I've missed you."

She paused before she said those last three words, giving him the impression that she might have changed what she was going to say at the last minute.

What did she expect from him? He felt a lick of anger and shoved it away. "I'm here now. Roll over, Emma."

Suddenly, he couldn't bear to look her in the face, couldn't stand to see the gaze that made *him* feel guilty… as if he had been the one to break her heart and not the other way around.

Rubbing her firm, round bottom, he leaned over her, tucking her hair across one shoulder and kissing the nape of her neck. When they were together in the past, he had never taken her like this. She had seemed too much the lady for a naughty position.

Or so he had thought. Maybe she had seen his naïveté as comical.

"Are you okay?" he asked, cursing inwardly that he felt the need to check.

She turned her head to smile at him with a mischievous look. "I won't break, Aidan. I swear."

He took her at her word. Checking her readiness with two fingers, he found her sex slick with moisture. She squirmed at his touch. Entering her slowly, he cursed. The fit was different from this angle, but no less stimulating. Sweat broke out on his forehead as he tried to pace his thrusts. The visual wasn't helping.

Emma's pale skin was luminous. Streetlights below cast a gentle glow through the thin curtains, so the room was never truly dark. He could see the curve where her waist dipped in and her hips flared.

Reaching beneath her, he palmed one breast, then the other. The flesh was full and firm. She wriggled backward, seating him more fully inside her. He was so close to coming every inch of skin all over his body was taut with expectation.

Suddenly, he knew it had to be different. If he and Emma had been long-time lovers, nothing would have been out of line. But they were neither lovers nor longtime. They were reconnecting with a tentative passion that left too much unspoken. She deserved to know he wanted *her*, not merely a faceless hookup.

Disengaging their bodies carefully, he moved her onto her back, lifted her leg over his hip and slid home again. She cried out and stared at him with a hazy expression, her lips parted, her breath coming quickly. Pleasure was the only emotion he recognized without question. And truly, he didn't want to examine the others too closely. Pleasure was fine. Pleasure was good. He didn't need to know what was going on inside her head.

Exhaustion lay heavy on his shoulders. If he had the

energy, he would move inside her forever. Feeling the butterfly caress when her sex squeezed his. Watching the way her breasts lifted and fell as her excitement grew. Touching her intimately, stimulating her little nerve center.

But the night had waned and he and Emma were half-sated from their earlier coupling. Even still, he managed to hold off for one more minute. "You enchant me," he said.

Emma frowned slightly. His statement held a hint of accusation, even to his own ears.

"I don't need you to talk, Aidan. Take us both where we want to go."

Closing his eyes, he heaved a deep breath and did just that…

When Emma awoke the next time, morning light filtered into her small bedroom. Aidan stood beside the bed, almost fully dressed. As she watched, he finished buttoning his shirt and tucked it into his pants.

She reared up on her elbows. "Are you leaving?"

He shot her a glance, nodding. "I promised Dylan and Mia that I would help them today out at the house. The whole crew is coming over for dinner tonight."

"Mia invited me, too."

She saw him go still, witnessed the rigid set of his shoulders. His reaction hurt, but she wasn't surprised.

No one needs to know about this.

Sitting up, she clutched her knees to her chest, the sheet protecting her modesty. "If you don't want me there tonight, I'll stay home."

He shrugged, still not meeting her eyes as he fastened his cuff links. "Go. Don't go. It's up to you."

"You don't have anything to worry about, Aidan. I won't embarrass you."

He slipped into his overcoat and buttoned it. "It's not a question of embarrassment. But my mother and Zoe and Mia get a real charge out of matchmaking. I don't want to get their hopes up."

"What does that mean?"

"I never bring women to Silver Glen. If they think you and I are an item, they'll hound me without mercy."

"Surely you've introduced them to women in the past."

"No."

She waited for him to continue, but that was all she was going to get.

He sat down on the edge of the bed and touched her cheek. "Thank you for last night. It was pretty damned incredible." Finally, she was able to see past his reserve to the genuine warmth and affection in his eyes.

Her face heated. "That must have been all you. My sexual prowess ranks one notch above old-maid schoolteacher."

Curling a hand behind her neck, he pulled her close for a long, sweet kiss. "Don't underestimate your appeal, Emma."

His tongue stroked hers gently, raising gooseflesh on her arms. What would he do if she threw herself into his embrace and begged him to stay? She mimicked his caress, no longer shy about letting him see what he did to her. When she bit his lip gently, teasing him with the sharp nip of her teeth, he rested his forehead on hers.

"Don't start something," he muttered.

She winnowed her fingers through the silky hair at the back of his head. "Why not? It's still early."

"You have a store to open, and I have to get home and take a shower."

"I have a shower," she pointed out.

"I'm wearing a tux, Emma. If I have to do the walk of shame, I'd rather get it over with before there are too many witnesses out and about."

"Ah." She pondered that. "You don't have a vehicle."

"I'll call Liam to come get me at the coffee shop down the street. He'll give me hell, but at least I won't have to walk back."

"It's not the walking that's a problem, is it? You don't want people to know you spent the night in town."

He shrugged. "Small communities thrive on gossip. I'd prefer to keep my affairs private."

"Is that what this is?" she snapped. "An affair?"

"I wasn't using that context, and you know it."

"Honestly, I don't understand much about you at all. You're an enigma, Aidan. My own personal sphinx. Once upon a time I thought I knew you inside and out. But no more."

"And whose fault is that?"

They had gone from hot kisses to bickering at warp speed.

"I take it the suspension of hostilities is over?" Stubborn, stubborn man. Why wouldn't he listen? "In case you forgot, *you* were the one who came to my bed, not the other way around."

"I don't want to fight with you," he said, shoulders slumped, his tone rough with fatigue.

"Fine. Then leave. And don't worry. When we see each other tonight, I'll act as if I barely know you. After all, it's the truth."

For long, heated seconds their gazes dueled. Hers angry and defiant, his stony with indifference or bitterness or both. When the standoff seemed at a stalemate and there were no more words to be said, he turned on his heel and strode out of the bedroom. Slamming the apartment door behind him, he left her, his rapid steps loud on the staircase down to the street.

She bowed her head, raking her hands through her hair. That certainly wasn't how she'd planned to end one of the best nights of her adult life. Why did she have to provoke him? Why couldn't she be satisfied with the knowledge that he had wanted her enough to show up in the middle of the night despite his better judgment?

The pillow beside her still carried the imprint of his head. She picked it up and sniffed the crisp cotton pillowcase, inhaling his scent…warm male and expensive cologne. For a brief time, it appeared that his enmity had vanished in the mist. Reconciliation had seemed possible.

Truthfully, she was spinning dreams out of thin air. Aidan was a man. He wanted sex. She was available.

There was no more to it than that. Maybe before he went back to New York he would relent and let her clear her conscience. But based on tonight, she wouldn't bet on it.

Aidan had to endure a merciless ribbing from his older brother in exchange for a ride up the mountain. Though Liam poked and prodded and did his best to ferret out information, Aidan wouldn't be moved. It was bad enough that he had caved to temptation and ended up in Emma's bed. He wouldn't compound his mistake by letting his family know the history he shared with one of Silver Glen's newest residents.

Fortunately, by the time he cleaned up and changed clothes and headed out to Dylan's place, Dylan and Mia were more than happy to see him. Cora was not in the best of moods. The housekeeper was in the kitchen cooking all the side dishes that would accompany the meal.

Dylan was still insisting on barbecuing despite the outside temperature.

"I'll bring it all inside," he said. "When everything is done. It's no big deal."

Mia glared at him, the baby on her hip. "You're the *host* tonight, Dylan. And this party was your idea. Just because it's family doesn't mean you can hide out by the grill."

Aidan inserted himself as peacemaker, raising his eyebrows. "I thought you were the party animal among us, bro," he said. "What's with this burning desire to play chef?"

Dylan snickered. "Burning. Get it? Maybe no one trusts me with raw meat. Is that the problem?"

Mia put her foot down. "I am your *almost*-bride, Dylan. And I'd really like a bubble bath, a glass of wine and some downtime, not necessarily in that order. Instead of dragging out the grill, why can't you let Aidan handle the barbecuing later so that you can entertain Cora for a little while?"

Aidan shrugged. "She has a point. I'm here to help. Why not take advantage of my culinary skills and kick back?"

"I've seen you cook," Dylan pointed out. "You have a tendency to burn water."

Mia wasn't impressed. She hugged Aidan. "Thanks for offering. And we accept." She handed a cranky Cora over to the baby's adoptive father. "Don't disturb me unless the house is on fire."

Aidan chuckled as he followed his brother back to the sunroom. "That woman of yours is a firecracker. Plain paper wrapper on the outside, but when you get her ticked off...*boom*."

"Are you saying my wife is plain?"

"God, no," Aidan said, backpedalling. "She's amazing, of course. I only meant that she seems quiet and shy until you get to know her."

Dylan made a sound something like a harrumph. In the middle of the cozy, sun-warmed den, he reclined on the floor with the baby, letting her climb over him like a play gym.

Aidan sprawled in a recliner, telling himself he wasn't envious. He didn't want kids. Though they were cute as hell. He had almost dozed off when Dylan's voice snapped him back to attention.

"So how long are you going to grieve, Aidan? Danielle has been gone a long time. She wouldn't want you to wear sackcloth and ashes forever. You've honored her memory. It's time to move on, don't you think?"

Aidan swung a foot lazily, his leg draped over the arm of the chair. "What I *think* is that my whole damned family can't mind their own business. Do I look like I need help with my love life?"

"Who knows? Whenever any of us visits you in New York, you pretend to be living like a monk in that fancy-ass apartment of yours."

"I didn't know I needed to introduce the occasional female guest to my extended family."

Dylan tickled Cora's tummy. "Is there really no one you can see yourself settling down with?"

Aidan shook his head in amazement. "I can't believe it. You and Liam get hitched and suddenly you're handing out advice to the lovelorn. I'm okay, I swear. My life is perfect. And if it's ever not perfect, you'll be the first to know. Now, can we drop it?"

His brother eyed him suspiciously. "There's something to be said for getting laid every night."

"Hell, Dylan. You're impossible. I'll have you know

I did have sex last night." As soon as the words left his mouth, he realized what he had done. *Crap*.

Dylan perked up like a retriever spotting a quail. "Say what?"

"Nothing. Forget I mentioned it."

Dylan rolled to his feet, holding Cora like a football. "Now I get it."

"Get what?"

"You look like you've been up all night. Liam told me he had to pick you up in town this morning. And that you had given him some lame excuse about an early morning walk."

"The two of you gossip more than a couple of old biddies. Have you checked your testosterone lately? I think you may be a quart low."

"Do we get to hear about her? Is it anyone I know?"

"Nothing happened. Nothing at all."

Eleven

Fortunately for Emma, her day was full. With the sun shining, Christmas shoppers were out in force. She and Mrs. Correll barely had time to take a breath in between customers.

Mia called midafternoon. "I wanted to make sure you were still coming to my house this evening," she said. "You left the party early last night, and I was afraid you were feeling bad."

Emma blushed, even though her friend couldn't see her. "I'm fine, honestly. I've been trying to pace myself." Except for the several hours last night she spent making love to Aidan instead of sleeping. "Do you need me to bring anything?"

"We've got enough food to feed half of North Carolina, but if you wouldn't mind coming an hour early, I'd love some help with my hair and makeup. Would that rush you too much?"

"Not at all. Mrs. Correll has offered to close up the shop today, so I can be there whenever you want me."

Emma had been to Dylan and Mia's house once before when she babysat little Cora. Even during this cold winter, she had to marvel at the home Dylan had built before he met Mia. The approach was a narrow lane flanked by weeping willows that in summer would create a foliage-lined tunnel. Today, though, the trees were sparse and bare.

As the house came into view, she sighed in envy. Dylan and his architect had created a magical, fairy tale of a place. The structure, built of mountain stone, dark timbers and copper, nestled amidst the grove of hardwood trees as if it had been there forever.

She parked in the area that had been roped off for cars and took one last look in the visor mirror. Coming face-to-face with Aidan was inevitable this evening, but even if they were going to ignore each other, she wanted to look her best.

The jersey dress she had ordered from England was comfortable and fit like a dream. The lace duster dressed it up and made the form-fitting fabric a bit more modest for a family dinner.

As she walked toward the front door, the unmistakable smell of meat cooking teased her nose, making her stomach growl. She'd grabbed a cup of yogurt for lunch, but that was a long time ago.

Mia answered the door herself. "Thank God you're here. Look what I've done to myself." She whipped the towel off her head.

Emma did her best to cover her shock, but it was bad. "Oh, dear…" She managed a smile. "We'll fix it. What did you do?"

"I was sick of having boring hair, and I didn't have time to make it to the salon, so I tried a home color—highlights actually. But all I got was this."

Emma winced inwardly. "Not to worry. But let's get started. We don't have much time."

Fortunately, the orangey red was mostly on the ends

of Mia's dark brown hair. Even so, this intervention was going to require desperate measures.

Aidan carried a tray of bison burgers into the kitchen and snagged a handful of potato chips before he went back out into the cold. Playing chef wasn't a bad gig, though. The down jacket he wore was plenty thick, and standing so close to the grill, even his hands were warm.

It wouldn't be long until his entire family came roaring down the lane. The momentary peace and quiet of a beautiful winter afternoon would get lost in the chaos. Even Cora was napping at the moment. And Dylan…who knew what Dylan was doing?

Seasoning and flipping meat didn't require much concentration. Aidan had plenty of time to think…and plenty to think about. Was Emma going to show up? Or had he been such an ass that she would decide to make an excuse to Mia and skip the whole thing?

He'd tried to speak to her before he came out to Dylan's. But when he parked in front of the antique shop, he could see through the window that her small business was packed with customers. Since he certainly didn't need an audience for a conciliatory conversation, he had put the car in gear and driven away.

After all, it wasn't as if anything he said to her last night wasn't true. But he felt bad for making her question her right to come to the party. She was Mia's friend, and Dylan and Mia could invite whomever they pleased to their dinner.

Aidan was the one with the problem, not Emma. Now, he had complicated his life even more by sleeping with the woman who had dropped back into his life so unexpectedly. Did he still wonder why she came to Silver Glen? Yes. Did he still want her? Yes.

The question was, what was he going to do about it? Already he felt himself softening toward her. Seeing her, talking to her, sleeping with her…all of that was dangerous. Clearly, Emma regretted the past. But he couldn't open himself up like that again.

Losing his father had left him to flounder in a world with too many temptations for a young boy. He'd missed his dad fiercely, but at the same time resented him for dying.

Aidan found Danielle in college and had latched on to her as if he had found his life's mate. But the magic had faded. That relationship ended in tragedy.

And then, there was Emma. Losing her had been the worst of all. He had learned his lesson. Emotional distance was key to his survival. Hats off to Liam and Dylan for committing to a future that held no guarantees. Aidan couldn't do it. Wouldn't do it. He'd had enough loss and suffering to last a lifetime.

He wanted Emma more than he wanted his next breath, but sharing her bed came with too many dangerous side effects. Emotions. Yearning. Hope. Hope for a different outcome this time.

If he had to go cold turkey to keep away from her, he'd simply have to do it. Last night had shown him a disturbing truth. He would never stop wanting Emma. And because being with her permanently was not in the cards, he had to protect himself. Even if Emma had some notion of getting back together—and that was a long shot—he was not interested.

He had to guard his impulses where she was concerned. Their interactions would take place only in public or amidst a crowd. That way he could avoid the temptation to share her bed again. He was a grown man, not a kid. Self-control was a product of maturity. Until it was time to go back to New York, celibacy was his friend.

The trouble was, everywhere he looked he could see her. In his mind's eye. Smiling at him. Flushed with pleasure. Arms outstretched to welcome him into her embrace. Her scent was in his head, the feel of her skin imprinted on his fingertips.

He poked at a half-done burger, scowling at it blindly. There was nothing special about Emma, other than her accent. If he still carried baggage from the past, it was only because he'd been an impressionable college kid, and she had made him feel like a man.

But he was smarter now. The sex last night was nothing out of the ordinary. No reason to think he was at risk for doing something stupid. He had enjoyed it, but it was over.

By the time Aidan finished his assigned task and carried the last of the main course into the kitchen, Dylan had come out of hiding and was talking to the housekeeper in between stealing bites of the appetizers. He took the heavy tray of meat from his brother. "Thanks, man. These look great."

"I guess we've got, what, twenty minutes until everyone shows up?"

"Maybe less. You know our crew. They can smell food from a mile away."

Before Aidan could respond, Emma appeared in the doorway. "I need to see you both in the living room, please."

Aidan frowned. "What's wrong?"

"Just come."

They followed her into the empty room. Emma, as always, looked effortlessly stylish. The form-fitting wine-colored dress she wore hugged her shape lovingly. If Aidan had his way, she would remove the lacy overdress thing so he could get a better look at her curves.

Dylan looked puzzled. "Where's Mia? I thought you were helping her get ready."

Emma wrinkled her nose and grimaced. "Mia had a little accident with some hair color." She fixed Dylan with a determined gaze. "You can't tease her about this, okay?"

"About what?"

"The color was dreadful, a cross between tomato-red and jack-o'-lantern-orange. We had no choice but to cut it off."

Aidan blanched. "You cut her hair?"

She shot him a look. "Not to worry. In boarding school we weren't allowed to go to the salon without our parents' permission. So anytime one of the girls wanted a new cut, I was the stylist."

Dylan firmed his jaw. "Is she crying? I want to see her."

Emma put a hand on his arm. "She's okay now. But the new 'do' is short. She wants you to see it before your guests arrive. But don't make a big deal, okay?" She turned to Aidan. "And when your family begins to show up, it would be nice if you could give them the same message."

"Of course."

Emma walked toward the bedrooms. "Hang on. I'll go get her."

Moments later a hesitant Mia appeared from around the corner. Her eyes went immediately to Dylan. "I feel like a fool." Her bottom lip trembled visibly.

Dylan put a hand over his heart. "Holy hell, woman. That is so hot." He went to her and feathered his fingers lightly over the ends of the pixie cut. "We may have to cancel the party," he said in a stage whisper, kissing the side of her neck.

Though Mia's eyes were pink-rimmed, she smiled and threw her arms around his neck. "I love you, Dylan."

He lifted her off her feet in a bear hug. "And I adore you, my sexy little fairy. Your hair is beautiful."

She pulled back, her gaze dubious. "You really think so?"

"I'll show you later," he muttered.

Aidan watched Emma, who was watching Mia and Dylan. On Emma's face was a wistful look that said she found the bridal couple's byplay romantic. Of course, that was a woman for you. Always suckers for a happy ending. Too bad those same women didn't realize life was seldom so tidy.

He glanced out the front window. "Car number one. Looks like Mom's. I'll go meet everybody if you two want a moment alone."

Mia smiled at him. "Thank you, Aidan, but I'm fine." She smoothed the skirt of her black dress, looking up at the man who would soon be placing a wedding ring on her finger. "Dylan and I are the hosts tonight. We should go greet our guests."

The two of them hurried away, arm in arm, leaving Aidan alone with Emma for the first time since he'd left her bed early that morning. "I stopped by to see you this afternoon," he said, "but the shop was really busy, so I didn't go in."

She perched on the arm of a chair. "I'm sorry I wasn't available."

"How's your head?"

"I'm still taking over-the-counter stuff for the head-ache, but it's not bad."

The stilted conversation was almost painful. Only hours ago they had been naked together. The mental image made his skin heat. "Last night was amazing, but it can't happen again."

"Why not?" She was pale, her expression mutinous.

"I'll be leaving soon. There's no future for us, Emma."

"Because you've decreed it?"

"Is that why you came here?" he asked. "To start over with me?"

"Not in the beginning. I was telling you the truth. I wanted to make my peace with you. To explain the past. But now that I've seen you again…now that we've made love…well, I have to wonder if there's something left between us. Something that never died."

"There isn't."

"Liar." She said it calmly, as if she could see inside the tortured recesses of his soul. "If you can kiss me and prove to me that you feel nothing at all for me, I'll leave you alone."

He held out his arms. "Do your best. It's sex, Emma. That's all. And I can get that from any woman. The young man you remember so fondly doesn't exist anymore."

"You're trying to make me angry by acting like a pig."

"Is it working?"

When she stood, the skin at his nape tingled. Emma on a mission was a formidable opponent. But he knew something she didn't. He knew that resisting temptation was not a choice. It was his only defense.

She crossed to where he stood and went nose-to-nose with him, although her nose was admittedly a few inches lower…almost at his collarbone, in fact.

He stared straight ahead, trying not to inhale her scent.

"This isn't fair," she complained. "I can't reach you. Sit down." She poked him in the chest until he took a step backward and sat down hard, hands behind him, on the edge of a beautiful oak table behind the sofa.

Now, their heights were much closer. The dress she wore had a scooped neck that revealed modest amounts of cleavage...but only if he let his gaze fall. His fingers gripped wood until pain shot up his wrists.

"Do your worst," he said, staring at her chin. His throat was so dry the words came out hoarse.

Emma leaned in. "You are a ridiculously handsome man," she murmured. "Gorgeous lips. Masculine. Sexy. Here goes..."

She pressed her mouth to his. Nothing happened except for his blood pressure shooting up about twenty points. *Focus. Focus.*

The first few seconds were barely a challenge. Her kiss was chaste, almost sweet. Nothing he couldn't handle.

Then she curled a hand behind his neck, her fingertips slipping inside the collar of his shirt to scrape deliberately across the bump at the top of his spine. *Sweet mother of God.*

Warm breath ticked his ear when she whispered. "How am I doing so far?"

He shrugged, his jaw so tight his head ached. "I've had better."

Emma's low chuckle was intensely sexual. He found himself getting hard despite his fierce concentration.

She came back to the kiss and put her all into it. When she nipped his bottom lip with sharp teeth, he gasped, giving her an opening to slide her tongue against his. Her taste went to his gut like raw liquor on an empty stomach. Hell, this was a pointless game.

He grabbed her close and angled her chin with one hand. The shock in her blue eyes gave him an enormous jolt of satisfaction. "You're an amateur," he said. "But I give you points for enthusiasm."

Then it was his turn. If he were going to admit defeat, he would drag her down with him. Pulling her fully into the V of his legs, he simply snapped. Everything he had tried to keep to himself, every needy, greedy urge to plunder, was unleashed.

Ten years of memories, of wondering, of futile anger and grief, coalesced into a white-hot need to make Lady Emma Braithwaite his. "Don't think you've won," he croaked. "This means nothing."

Her eyes brimmed with moisture, the look on her face a mixture of tenderness and wonder. "I understand," she said quietly. "Whatever you say, Aidan. Whatever you want."

Cupping her breast in his hand, he stroked the nipple through its soft covering. "I want you. Now."

Before Emma could say a word in denial or consent, a loud noise nearby shattered the mood, the one sound guaranteed to stifle a man's ardor.

Maeve's Kavanagh's cheerful greeting…"We're all here. Let the party begin."

Twelve

For Emma, the next two hours took on a surreal quality. The mood in the house was joyful and rowdy, rightly so. The Kavanaghs en masse created a special kind of magic. One of their own was tying the knot, and in true Irish fashion, they were prepared to party all night.

Despite Emma's efforts to stay in the background, Mia insisted on making sure she met everyone individually. The festive gathering at the hotel had been much larger and more formal. Tonight, however, was a time for one-on-one conversations, sibling jokes and eating.

Emma had been taken aback at the amount of food laid out buffet-style, sure they would never consume half of it. But she had underestimated the appetite of a full-grown Kavanagh male. Amidst much good-natured jostling and name-calling everyone filled his or her plate and found a seat.

Dylan's mission-style dining room table, with leaves inserted, was big enough to handle the whole crew in one sitting. Emma took a spot at the far end and across the table from Aidan. She had promised not to embarrass him, and despite what had happened moments before the party began, she was determined not to give anyone cause to think she and Aidan were a couple.

Her interactions with him were complicated enough

already without other people butting in and offering their opinions. Apparently Aidan had come to the same conclusion, because he barely acknowledged Emma's presence. It was Mia who offered her a seat, Mia who involved her in the conversations that bounced back and forth during the meal.

Cora sat in a high chair at one corner, her chubby cheeks red with excitement. It was probably too much stimulation for a little one near bedtime, but Dylan and Mia had wanted to include her.

Each of the younger Kavanagh men had brought a date. As far as Emma could tell, the females in question were casual connections at best, because all four of them had to be introduced to the group.

The only unattached members of the dinner party were Maeve and Cora, Aidan and Emma. At first, Emma was on edge. But when she realized that no one was inclined to ask awkward questions, she relaxed.

It was almost unbelievable that every single one of Aidan's siblings was tall, broad-shouldered and dangerously attractive. The deceased Mr. Kavanagh must have been a fine figure of a man. Only the youngest, James, looked more like his mother.

Emma had been reared in *polite* society. By the time she was ten, she knew how to comport herself at an afternoon tea or a grown-up dinner party. Although tonight's gathering was much less stuffy, the Kavanaghs were a sophisticated lot, well traveled, well read and comfortable with the trappings of wealth.

The discussions of books, movies, politics and the world in general were stimulating. After a while, Emma felt comfortable enough to jump in and be a part of the occasional debate. Aidan, on the other hand, remained oddly silent. He nodded and answered when asked a direct question, but he was content to nurse a beer and observe the proceedings with a small smile on his face. From where Emma sat, his little grin seemed to encompass love for his family and an enjoyment of their eccentricities.

When the housekeeper took Cora, ready to put her to bed, Liam held up a hand. "One moment please, Gertie." He stood and picked up his wineglass. "We're gathered here tonight to celebrate the upcoming marriage of my brother Dylan to the beautiful and much-too-good-for-him Mia."

A wave of laughter greeted his statement.

He carried on, looking at Mia with warmth and affection. "Mia…when my brothers and I asked Dylan what kind of bachelor party he wanted tonight, his answer was *none*."

Dylan's face turned red. He ducked his chin.

Liam shook his head, smiling. "He told us everything in the world he wanted was under this very roof. And that the two days when you and Cora become official Kavanaghs will be the happiest of his life."

Every female around the table, Emma included, gave an audible sigh…*awwww*. For the first time during the meal, Aidan looked straight at Emma and rolled his eyes with a humorous expression. She shrugged, not about to apologize for appreciating romance.

"To Mia and Dylan." Liam held his glass toward the happy couple. The toast echoed around the table.

"To Mia and Dylan."

Maeve had tears in her eyes as she gave Cora a quick kiss. When the housekeeper departed with the baby, Maeve remained standing. "This is a party," she said. "So I won't belabor the point. But I want to say that I have the most wonderful sons in the world. And adding

Zoe and Mia to our family has been a joy." She paused, moving her gaze from Aidan to Gavin, Patrick, Conor and James. "But the rest of you…"

The men all groaned, as if they knew what was coming next.

Maeve ignored their response. "I'm not getting any younger," she said, managing to look frail and needy despite the fact that she was a vibrant woman in perfect health. "You young women be careful. The Kavanagh male is a slippery species. I'd love to have half a dozen grandchildren while I'm still able to enjoy them."

Catcalls and hoots and hollers ended her pseudo-pitiful speech. Laughter erupted again as she was forced to sit down in defeat. But the broad smile on her face told Emma she was perfectly happy to sit back and watch her sons find worthy matches.

Emma wondered if she understood exactly how unlikely that was in Aidan's case.

By unanimous consent, the group moved to the large, comfortable living room. A roaring fire warmed the space and cast a circle of intimacy. Again, Emma stayed far away from Aidan.

This time the conversation turned to less personal topics. Gavin's date mentioned spending Christmas in Zurich with her family. Emma, seated beside her, sighed. "It sounds like a wonderful trip. I've heard the skiing there is awesome. Actually, now that I've moved to Silver Glen, I was hoping to learn how to ski myself."

Without warning, a dead hush fell over the group. Like Sleeping Beauty's castle under a wicked spell, everyone in the room froze. What had Emma said? She replayed her innocent statements in her head. They hardly seemed the kind of words to provoke such a response. Though the women who sat with Aidan's younger brothers appeared confused, no one could miss the uneasy silence. The expressions on Kavanagh faces ranged from dismay to outright alarm.

Maeve suddenly looked her age, and Mia's distress was palpable. *What did I do?* Emma wondered frantically. In desperation, she looked to Aidan for help. He stood up, never once looking her way, his face carved in granite. "If you'll excuse me..."

No one said a word as he left the room. Thirty seconds later, the front door of the house opened and closed quietly.

Emma swallowed. "I'm sorry," she said. "But what just happened?"

Liam heaved a sigh, his expression a combination of resignation and worry. "Come with me to the kitchen, Emma."

She followed him out of the room with her heart thumping like mad. When they were out of earshot, she leaned against the sink. "What in the heck is going on? What's wrong with Aidan?"

"It's not your fault." Liam ran both hands through his hair. "You stepped on an emotional land mine."

"I don't understand."

"Aidan never comes home at Christmas. When he was younger, he brought his fiancée to Silver Glen at the holidays to meet the family. While they were here, she and Aidan went skiing. Danielle fell and hit her head. She died forty-eight hours later without ever waking up from a coma."

"Oh, my God." Emma's stomach heaved. "I'm so sorry."

"You had no way of knowing. He's been on edge since he left New York. Coming here...in December...has been a strain. But he wouldn't miss Dylan's wedding."

"I'm going to go talk to him."

"Probably not a good idea. When a man is hurting, he wants to hide and lick his wounds."

"I've ruined the party, Liam. I should go."

Liam touched her shoulder. "Nothing is ruined, Emma. Aidan will be okay. He needs a little time to re-group, that's all."

Mia wandered into the kitchen, her face troubled. "Did Liam tell you?"

Emma nodded, her throat too tight to answer.

Mia hugged her and then stepped back. "I should have warned you, I guess. Dylan told me how bad it was back then. My heart breaks for Aidan. He's never been seri-ous about anyone since."

"I see." Emma swallowed hard, on the verge of tears. "Thank you for inviting mc tonight," she whispered. "I'm going to see if I can find him and apologize."

"It might make things worse," Liam said.

He was probably right, but Emma couldn't bear the thought of Aidan wandering cold and alone on a night that was supposed to be a celebration. "Maybe," she said. "But I have to try."

Mia nodded. "I'd want to do the same."

"Please tell Dylan I'm sorry," Emma said.

"Don't be ridiculous. I'm so glad you were here. Mom and Dad and my friends from Raleigh aren't arriving until a few hours before the ceremony tomorrow, so it's been nice having some emotional backup."

"Hey," said Liam, his tone aggrieved. "*We* love you."

Mia kissed his cheek. "I know you do. But sometimes a woman needs a break from all that testosterone."

Emma walked to where her vehicle was parked, her feet crunching on the frost-covered grass. The truth was, she had no good plan to look for Aidan...none at all. When she made it back to town, she cruised the darkened streets, trying to spot his fancy sports car. She even made a pass through the parking lot of the Silver Dollar Saloon. But no Aidan.

Driving up the mountain was her last shot. Aidan was staying at the lodge, true, but there was at least a possibility that he had left town. When she handed her keys to the valet and stepped out, she shivered. The wind had picked up, making the night seem even colder. She bundled her coat around her, hurrying up the steps of the hotel.

In the lobby, she paused. Aidan might be outside, though it was unlikely. The young man working the desk tonight was an employee she didn't recognize, so that might be to her advantage.

She approached him casually, removing her coat and straightening her dress and duster. "Hello," she said, beaming him a bright smile. "I'm trying to catch up with Mr. Kavanagh, Aidan Kavanagh," she clarified. "Did you happen to see him go up to his room earlier?"

The barely twenty-something blinked, seeming dazzled by her deliberately cozy manner. "Yes, ma'am," he said. "About an hour ago. May I ring his room for you?"

Emma reached in her purse and pressed a large bill into his hand. "No, thank you. He's expecting me."

Leaving the flustered clerk to ponder the fact that he might have been indiscreet, Emma headed for the elevator. She had no clue what she was going to say to Aidan or how she could make things better, but she had to try. The memory of his face as he left the party hurt her deeply.

Stepping out of the elevator, she paused a moment. The elegant hallway was quiet. It was possible that some guests had retired for the night, though unlikely. Even still, she didn't have the luxury of making a scene.

At Aidan's door, she knocked softly and listened for any sound inside his room. Nothing. Knocking harder, she held her breath, praying that he wouldn't ignore her.

At last, she was pretty sure she heard him on the other side of the door. She knocked a third time. "I know you're in there, Aidan. Let me come in. Please."

Thirteen

Aidan unlocked the door with a sense of fatalism and swung it open, stepping back to allow Emma to enter. She would not leave until she was satisfied that he was okay. It was his own damned fault for reacting so viscerally to her innocent observations. But somehow, the thought of Emma on a ski slope had made his heart stop and his stomach revolt.

No surprise, really, given his past with her. But she didn't need to know that. His job now was to convince her that he was fine…that he'd had a momentary crisis, but it had passed.

He saw her glance at the whiskey decanter. "I'm not drowning my sorrows," he said, leaning heavy on the sarcasm.

"I didn't say that."

"But you were thinking it."

She removed her coat and tossed it on a chair. Only hours before he had been holding her, his body taut with need. What he wouldn't give to rewind the clock and pretend this evening had never happened.

"I'm so sorry, Aidan."

He shrugged, her sympathy about as comfortable to him as a hair shirt. "It's no big deal. I was caught off guard, that's all."

And stunned at the thought that you could die...just like poor Danielle.

"It was more than that, and you know it." She cupped his face in her hands, her eyes filled with tears. "I can't imagine how horrible it must have been for you... losing someone you loved that way. No wonder Christmas is a bad time."

He couldn't bear her touch. Not now. He was raw inside. "Feel free to go," he said, pushing her hands away along with her gentle empathy. "As you can see, I'm neither drunk nor high and I have no plans to harm myself in a dramatic show of grief."

Turning his back, he paced the room, wondering how long it would take to get rid of her. The longer she stayed, the more he wanted her. And he'd done enough stupid things for one night.

Emma curled up in a chair. "Tell me about Danielle," she said softly. "What was she like?"

He continued to traverse the room, in danger of wearing a path in the carpet. Talking to Emma about Danielle was both ironic and terribly sad. "She was delightful," he said, casting back for memories. "A good person in every sense of the word. She threw herself into life with abandon—charming, funny, always kind to those who were out of step with the world."

"She sounds like a lovely woman."

"She was. I never heard her say an unkind word about anyone."

"How long had the two of you been together?"

"Four years."

Emma winced visibly. "And the accident?"

He didn't want to go there. But that moment was as vivid in his mind as if it had happened yesterday. Some days he thought he would never be able to erase the recollection. So why did it matter if he told Emma at least part of the truth?

"Liam told you, I guess, that I brought Danielle home to meet my family. It was December, and the town was decked out for the holidays. Danielle fell in love with Silver Glen."

"That doesn't surprise me. Who could resist?"

"True. At any rate, we had been here a couple of days when we got a surprise. An early snowfall, almost six inches. Conor and I were jazzed. We made plans to go skiing and took Danielle with us."

"Had she skied before?"

"She knew *how* to ski, but she wasn't very good at it, and it had been a long time. So we kept to the easy runs, not quite the bunny slopes, but close. She regained her confidence finally, and we decided to tackle something a little more challenging. Conor went first. Then Danielle. I brought up the rear. About halfway down, she lost her balance and careened off the course, headed for a clump of trees. I heard her laughing, and then she screamed, and then she crumpled in a broken heap on the ground."

He wasn't looking at Emma as he struggled through the dark tale. So he was startled when he felt her arms come around him.

She pressed her cheek to his chest. "I can't even imagine what you went through. How dreadful."

"We got her down the mountain with the help of the ski patrol, but she was unconscious. At the hospital, they determined that the blow to her head had caused a massive brain bleed. She never woke up. Two days later, she was dead."

Emma hugged him so tightly he thought his ribs would crack. He rested his chin on the top of her head. He knew Emma was crying...for him. He wished he could cry, too. But he had buried his wounds and his emotions so deeply they were fossilized.

"There's more," he said, the two words hoarse.

She took him by the hand and drew him to the sofa. He sprawled in the corner and draped an arm around her shoulders when she nestled close.

"You don't have to do this," she said. "I've heard enough."

"But not the worst part. There's something I've never told anyone."

"You can trust me with your secret." She squeezed his hand.

"I was the one who thought Danielle should come with us. I'll never forget asking her. She was curled up by the fire—wrapped in a cozy afghan, reading. I told her the plan, but she said for me to go on with my brother...that she was perfectly happy to sit with her book and enjoy a quiet morning."

Emma moved restlessly, perhaps sensing what was to come. But she didn't speak.

"I'm to blame," he said, shuddering inwardly. "I begged her to go with us. Told her how much fun it would be. And in the end, I won her over."

"Oh, Aidan."

He ignored the loaded comment.

"It was my fault she died. I have to live with that."

Emma sat in silence, her world in ashes. Aidan hadn't lied to her after all. When he told her the sex was only sex, it had been the truth. Because he was still in love with his dead fiancée.

He might not realize it. But she heard the emotional pain in his words...heard him describe Danielle with such love and affection. And because his grief was so all-encompassing and so deep, he had been unable to move on.

Clearly, coming to Silver Glen at Christmas for his brother's wedding was a decision he had made at great personal cost. Every Christmas tree and wreath and sprig of holly must be a bitter reminder of all he had lost.

His reaction, more than anything, told Emma she'd never had a chance at rekindling their old romance. There was nothing to rekindle. She was the only one who had kept the glow of a youthful relationship alive. For a man to love so faithfully and so well that he still grieved years later and continued to carry a load of guilt, meant that his heart was not his own. He had buried it with Danielle.

She cleared her throat. "Thank you for telling me. She must have been a very special woman."

Suddenly, everything seemed awkward. Should she go…leave him to his own devices? Or should she stay to give him comfort…any kind of comfort she could offer?

Aidan sat up and rested his elbows on his knees, his head in his hands. "Did I upset Dylan and Mia?"

Emma chose her words carefully. "If you're asking was the party ruined…no. But of course your family is worried about you. We could go back if you want."

"God, no." His rough laugh held no humor at all. "I did enough damage earlier. I'm sure they don't need me throwing a damper on things. I'll have an early night, and tomorrow I'll make it up to them somehow. I feel like an idiot."

She touched his arm. "You're a man who cares deeply. Nothing wrong with that." Since she still had not resolved her inner struggle, she rose to her feet. "I should go now. I'll see you at the wedding tomorrow." She put a hand on his shoulder. "I'm really sorry. About Danielle, I mean."

He stood and faced her. "Will you think it incredibly crass if I ask you to stay tonight?"

She searched his eyes, looking for any indication that he truly wanted her. Was it enough to know that she would be giving him comfort in a way no one else could at the moment? "I thought you said physical intimacy between the two of us was a bad idea."

"It's been a hell of an evening. Being rational is not high on my list at the moment. But you're free to say no. I would say no to me if I were you."

The humor was weak, but it was there. He had turned a corner. "I don't believe saying *no* to you is my strong suit."

He curled a strand of her hair around his finger. "I want to make one thing clear before we go any further..."

"Okay." She braced inwardly.

"When I went all psycho tonight, it wasn't only because I was remembering Danielle's accident. It was also a gut-deep reaction to the idea that you could get hurt. You mean something to me, Emma. Maybe it's not what it was in the past, and maybe it's not what you deserve, but I do have feelings, despite my efforts to the contrary."

Her heart warmed more than it should have. His eyes were filled with *something*. Affection? Attraction? What self-respecting female went to bed with a man who was in love with another woman? Was she a masochist?

"You mean something to me as well. But you should know that I don't expect anything beyond tonight. I want to be with you. If that brings us both pleasure, that's reason enough."

Fourteen

Aidan was so deeply enmeshed in his lies of omission that he couldn't even *reach* the moral high ground, much less stand on it. He was too busy protecting himself from Emma. And now…tonight…with deliberate intent, he was going to take what she was offering and damn the consequences.

When Emma mentioned skiing earlier, it *did* bring back the past and Danielle's accident. But what had really prompted his abrupt departure was a vicious jolt of panic at the thought that the world could lose Emma as well.

For the last ten years, in the midst of anger and grief and frustration with himself for still caring about her, at least he had known that somewhere on the planet she was alive and well.

He hadn't truly realized until this evening that if she were to die, he couldn't bear it. Emma married to another man and happy with babies? That, he could wrap his head around. But dead? Like Danielle? The notion was unfathomable.

Gripping one of her wrists, he reeled her into his embrace. "I have fantasies about your hair," he muttered.

"My hair?" A little squiggle of a frown appeared between her brows. "Surely you can do better than that."

"Oh, no," he said, drawing her toward the bedroom

before she could change her mind. "It's a guy thing. The more you pin and twist and tuck it, the more I want to muss you up."

She laughed softly. "Be my guest. This fancy updo is giving me a headache anyway."

Once they crossed the threshold into the inner room of the suite, he closed the door and leaned against it. A single small lamp cast an intimate circle of light. Emma eyed him warily, perhaps wondering if he were in his right mind. Maybe he was and maybe he wasn't. Ever since the moment he came face-to-face with her in the emergency room, he had questioned his sanity.

Ten years ago she had betrayed him and made a fool of him, and yet at the same time she had been the center of his world for three amazing months. Now, the good memories battled the bad, as if trying to convince him that the past was the past…that the future held endless possibilities.

Emma had asked again and again for the chance to explain her actions. To make amends. To request absolution. He had shut her down every time she tried.

Should he let her speak of that terrible day? Let her attempt to make sense of it? Or did it even matter from the vantage point of a decade in time? He was a man. He understood that life included disappointments. The blessings of family and friends were balanced with the inevitable struggles of living. Not that all struggles were as tragic as Danielle's death.

Shaking his head slightly, he decided such questions could wait. Emma wasn't going anywhere. Maybe he would let her open the door to the past. But not here. And not now.

"Come closer, my English rose," he muttered, unbuttoning his shirt and pulling it free of his pants. When he shrugged out of it and tossed it toward the closet, Emma's eyes widened.

She sighed, lips parted, as she obeyed his command. Placing her hands flat on his chest, she flicked his flat, copper-colored nipples with sharp fingernails. The tiny stings of pain arrowed to his groin and joined the rush of arousal that already had his sex lifting to attention.

"I won't regret this," she said softly. "I'm glad we had this chance to see each other again. Maybe we both needed closure."

He didn't like the finality in her description, even though he'd been the one to say they had no future. "You talk too much," he said, only half-joking. He didn't want to *think* tonight. All he wanted was to feel her body straining against his.

Without asking, he pulled the pins from her hair one at a time and dropped them into a crystal dish. Each small *clink* was quiet music to his ears. When he was done, he used both hands to winnow through her hair, separating the strands and smoothing the wavy tresses. "That's better," he said softly.

The prelude to sex was easier this time, more natural. Removing Emma's clothes was a reverent task not to be rushed. When he had her down to a set of ultrafeminine undies and bra, he finished his own disrobing. Lowering the zipper on his slacks was tricky. His erection bobbed thick and eager as he eased it free of confinement.

Together, they climbed into the enormous hedonistic bed. The Silver Beeches Lodge spared no expense when it came to their guests' comfort. Whether for sleep or more intimate pursuits, the bedding and mattress provided an island of physical bliss.

He leaned over Emma on one elbow, studying the dewy perfection of her skin. Maybe something about the air and water in the British Isles produced this exquisite variety of female.

"Tell me one of *your* fantasies," he said. "Something naughty you've always wanted to do but never had the chance."

Her instant, cheeky grin made him shiver. She sighed. "I've always wanted to have sex in a lift."

"A lift?" All the blood in his head had rushed south, making him slow to comprehend.

"You know…an elevator. Preferably one with glass on the top half. So people watching might have a clue as to what's happening, but wouldn't know for sure."

He gaped at her. "Emma. You wicked girl."

Her shrug was epic. "You asked."

"So I did." And now all he could think about was where such an elevator might exist. Certainly not in the town of Silver Glen. "I'm going to forget you said that," he muttered. "Although getting the image out of my head will be hard."

"You said *hard*." She snickered. "Is that a Freudian slip?"

He touched her smooth thigh, running his hand from her knee to the crevice where leg joined torso. Her underwear was tiny and sexy. Twisting a finger in the side band, he snapped it deliberately. "Freud might want to study my caveman tendencies." Tugging the small piece of fabric to uncover her secrets, he nudged her hip. "Lift your butt."

Now she was completely bare from the waist down. He took the opportunity to tease her with kisses that ranged from playful to deliberately sexual.

Emma moved restlessly, her hands gripping his head. "Aidan."

"Hmmm…?" Her taste was exquisite.

"I want to do something."

"Pretty sure we're already doing it."

"I'm serious."

He winced when she pulled his hair. "Okay, okay." Rolling to his back, he turned his head to look at her. "You have my attention."

Emma, in turn, surprised the hell out of him by moving agilely and straddling his waist. "I want to take care of you tonight," she said. "Will you let me?"

Her body was a pleasant weight at his hips. "I'm not sure what you mean."

She leaned forward, her lace-covered breasts in kissing distance, and took his wrists in her hands. "I want you to grab hold of the spindles in the headboard. We don't have anything to tie you with, so you'll have to promise not to let go."

A fresh current of arousal flooded his veins. "Please don't tell me being a dominatrix is on your bucket list. I'll never believe it." People often made jokes in tense situations. This definitely counted. "A lady never acts out of character," he said. "I think you've been reading too many erotic novels."

"I'm not always a lady, Aidan. Perhaps you don't know me as well as you think."

Well, hell's bells. That shut him up. With her small hands guiding his wrists, he found the slender pieces of wood and wrapped his fingers around two of them. The stretch in his shoulders was pleasant. So far.

"What next?" he asked, trying to gauge her mood.

Emma shifted her weight back to his hips again. Her expression defied analysis. Not uncertainty. More like assessment. He wasn't sure if that aroused him or worried him. In all honesty, a bit of both.

"Are you comfortable?" she asked, her hands flat on

her thighs. Considering that her lady parts were tantalizingly close to his rigid sex, it was a loaded question.

"Yes."

She nodded once. "Good. Now close your eyes."

"Um…" He flexed his feet, his toes cold.

"Are you afraid of me, Aidan?" Her question could have been flirtatious, but the tone suggested she was serious.

"Should I be?" he asked, dodging the truth.

"I want to make you feel good…that's all. No need for alarm. You can trust me."

He wondered if this were some kind of test. To prove to him that she had changed. "I'm in your hands. Be gentle with me."

His half-hearted teasing didn't even coax a smile from her. "I'm waiting for you to close your eyes." She said it patiently in the tone of someone dealing with a stubborn toddler.

"Are you going to ditch the bra?" he asked hopefully. The pastel lace was mostly transparent, but that didn't mean he didn't want to uncover what was underneath. He simply hadn't gotten to it when she turned the tables so unexpectedly.

Emma shrugged. "It won't matter," she said softly. "You won't be able to see."

The simple statement struck him as a threat, even though there was nothing of menace in the words. Apparently, his trust issues went deeper than he realized. Now that he thought about it, he'd never allowed any woman this kind of physical control.

He'd played naughty games with females in the past, but Aidan had always wielded the power. From this side of the metaphorical whip, he felt distinctly uneasy. But he wasn't about to reveal his reservations. Not at this particular moment.

Inhaling a deep gulp of air that lifted his chest, he let it out slowly as he closed his eyes and tightened his grip.

Fifteen

Aidan Kavanagh was an extraordinarily masculine and beautiful man. Though he had complied with her orders, Emma sat motionless for a moment, enjoying the tableau. His skin was lightly tanned, the hair on his torso and beneath his arms a shade darker than his deep brown locks with the hint of fire in them.

With his arms extended above his head, she could see the tendons and muscles that delineated his strength. Broad shoulders and a hair-dusted chest tapered to a trim waist, flat stomach and below...*Oh, lordy...*

His sex, though still somewhat turgid, lay against his thigh. Perhaps her offer to make him feel good was ambiguous enough to make it difficult for him to relax.

"I'm going to start with a massage," she said quietly.

Aidan made no response, but he muttered something inaudible.

Scooting up onto his chest, she leaned forward until she could reach his wrists. Pressing her thumbs to his pulse, she dug into his flesh and ran a path all the way to the crook of his elbows. Then, using both hands on one arm at a time, she worked her way from his elbow to his upper arm.

Perhaps because of the posture she insisted he adopt, his shoulder muscles were tight. She spent some time there, finding knots and working them out. It might have been easier if he had been on his stomach, but she wanted to watch his face.

At one point, he flinched. "Too hard?" she asked. One of her college friends had studied sports medicine, and Emma had picked up tips from her. But sometimes people couldn't take too firm a pressure.

"Your *assets* are in my face."

"Ah." She blushed, though he couldn't see her. "Almost done with this part." She moved on to his neck and behind his ears. As her hands warmed his skin, she inhaled the smell of him…the yummy *guy* aroma that made a girl's knees weak and led to all sorts of improper thoughts.

The next bit was very personal. Letting her fingertips glide gently, she feathered her way across his forehead, down his nose and cheeks, along his chin and over his firm jaw to his throat.

Aidan's Adam's apple bobbed visibly when she pressed lightly where his pulse beat in the side of his neck. Moving to his collarbone, she stroked it slowly. As she shifted back a couple of inches so she could reach his chest, she realized that his sex was no longer at rest. It was firm and erect and bumped her bottom eagerly.

From this particular angle, she could have joined their bodies easily. But there was time for that later. She concentrated on rubbing his chest, tracing his rib cage, following the line of his sternum.

She saw his tongue come out to wet his lips. It seemed as if his breathing had picked up in tempo. At one time, she'd had the freedom to touch Aidan however and whenever she wanted, knowing that every brush of skin made them both drunk with happiness and arousal.

For one painful moment, the stab of grief consumed

her. Even if Aidan eventually forgave her for the past, they would never be the same two people. What they had shared at Oxford was exhilarating. They had been young and in love and frightfully full of themselves.

Determined to forget the past, she moved quickly, avoiding Aidan's straining erection and settling in between his legs. She heard him curse, possibly because he thought she had been preparing to join their bodies by sliding down onto his shaft.

She crouched on her knees. Avoiding his groin area, she rubbed his hipbones. His thighs were next, then his bony knees, his calves, his ankles and finally his big feet. When she slid her fingers between his toes, his back arched off the bed.

"Enough," he wheezed.

"I'm trying to relax you. These are standard massage techniques."

"Screw that." He sat up, raking his hands through his hair. His eyes glittered with desire. "Either your technique sucks, or when you touch me I go insane. I'm betting on the latter."

"Oh." She'd been trying to calm him, to make him feel good after a crappy evening. "I didn't even touch your..."

"My penis?" he offered helpfully.

Frowning at him, she eased back onto her bottom and pretzeled her legs. "I don't like that word."

"It's a perfectly good word...unless you prefer di—"

She slapped a hand across his mouth. "I prefer not to talk about it at all. I'm more into *doing*."

One side of his mouth kicked up in a grin. "Happy to oblige." He mimicked her position, then took her hands and tucked them around his shaft. "Feel free to massage this poor neglected body part."

It was her turn to swallow. His sex was proportionally large, the shaft veined and strong, the head weeping for her. "I don't think they covered this in the manuals," she muttered.

When she ran her thumb beneath the flange and used her other hand to squeeze, Aidan's eyes rolled back in his head. Well, they might have. She didn't exactly know since his face was scrunched up and his lashes fanned out against his cheeks.

So far, so good. "You really are tense," she breathed.

Despite his advanced state of arousal, Aidan laughed, opening his eyes to look at her with a glazed expression. "*Tense* doesn't even begin to describe it. You have an unfair advantage with that upper crust British accent. Everything out of your mouth sounds like a sexual come-on."

"Close your eyes, naughty boy," she said, channeling her old headmistress. "I'm not done yet."

Emma might not be done, but Aidan was almost there. His skin was so sensitive to the touch that it hurt. He took her hand and removed it from the trigger. "Not like this, Emma. I want to be inside you."

Her lower lip pouted the tiniest bit. "I wanted to make you feel good," she said.

He groaned, shaking his head in bemusement. "Mission accomplished. Now turn around."

"Why?"

"Don't you trust me?"

"Not funny, Kavanagh."

"Don't be so prissy. I'm only going to undo you." When she gave him her back, he unfastened the band of her bra carefully and slid the straps down her shoulders. "There. Now was that so bad?"

She faced him again, her breasts high and firm and

beautiful. Although she had been bold when his eyes were closed, now she seemed hesitant…even shy. He cupped one breast in his hand. "You don't have to stay. I'm fine." Why he was giving her the chance to leave, he wasn't sure. But it seemed somehow important.

She took his free hand and held it to her cheek. "I don't want to leave, Aidan."

"Are you staying because you feel sorry for me?" The thought of her sympathy chafed.

But she shook her head vigorously. "I'd be lying if I said yes. I really did want to make you feel better, but the real reason is selfish."

He cocked his head. "Tell me. Please."

Pale, narrow shoulders lifted and fell. "I want to feel it again."

"It?"

"The high. At the risk of giving you a swelled ego, you're very good at satisfying a woman sexually."

Her explanation was not what he expected to hear. It seemed impersonal and cold. Though paradoxically, he and Emma were anything but at the moment. Hunger sizzled between them. It seemed, however, as if they were reading from a script, both of them afraid to speak the truth.

Refusing to acknowledge her confession, bogus or not, he took her with him under the covers. Their arms and legs tangled. "I want you, Emma. You have no idea how much."

She nestled against him. "I want you, too, Aidan."

Still, he felt dissatisfied. Perhaps this was payback for the way he had insisted that anything physical between them was *only* sex. Who had he been trying to convince? Emma had asked him if there was still a spark. He had denied it. But with her here in his bed, he seemed like the worst kind of liar.

He ran his hands over her back, tracing her spine, feeling the press of her breasts against his chest. If he closed his eyes, he could pretend he was twenty-one again. Eager. Painfully naive about women. Standing on the precipice of a moment that would change his life forever.

How could he have made such a wrong choice? Such a desperately wrong choice? He'd been hurt, true. But he liked to think he was wiser now. Even in the face of Emma's betrayal, he should have fought for her.

Her cheek rested trustingly against his chest. Could she feel his heart thump? To him, it felt like a runaway train. Beating out a rhythm on the tracks.

Last chance. Last chance. Last chance.

Confusion and lust were poor bedfellows. Lust won every time, even in the absence of clear thinking. He moved over her and kissed her roughly. She arched into his embrace, giving him everything. Her softness. Her kindness. Her capacity for loving.

Love. The word was so damned dangerous. As he entered her with one hard thrust, he felt the syllable reverberate in his head, in his heart, in his loins. He did not love her. He wouldn't allow it. Never again.

But as his body stroked into hers, as her arms linked around his neck, binding him to her, he felt his will crumble. How could this be wrong? How could anything this good be wrong?

They loved wildly, passionately, battling almost to see who could give the other more pleasure. He lost the ability to speak, to reason, to keep her at bay.

He wanted everything she was, everything *he* was when he was with her. Emotions he had denied for years washed over him, drowning every one of his stupid life rules. His need for release bore down on him, but he didn't want this to end. He wanted to love her all night long.

When Emma cried out his name, though, shuddering beneath him, he had no choice but to follow her. The intensity of his climax tore him apart and rebuilt him cell by cell.

Eons later, he clutched her close and slept. But it was a fitful slumber. He jerked awake, time and again, dreaming that he had lost her. In his nightmares, he stood inside a train car, watching her wave to him as some immoveable force carried him away.

After the third time when he awoke sweating and trembling, he eased from the bed and went in search of a drink of water. He stood naked in the living room area of the suite and peered out at the night between a crack in the drapes. The world was still and dark.

Today was his brother's wedding day. Dylan was gaining a wife and a daughter in one fell swoop. What must it be like to know that people depended on you? That their health and well-being directly impacted your own happiness?

In Dylan's shoes, Aidan would be scared to death. That was a hell of a thing for a grown man to admit. Even now, with Emma asleep in the other room, Aidan had to resist the urge to run. He remembered his early twenties all too well. He'd been a mess. Drinking too much. Sleeping with too many women. Teaching himself not to feel.

All because Emma Braithwaite's betrayal had crushed him. The pain had made it hard to breathe. And it had made him stupid. Unfortunately, Danielle had borne the brunt of that.

His breath fogged the glass. Rubbing his thumb across the condensation, he told himself to let go of the memories. But what was the old saying? He who forgets the past is doomed to repeat it?

Aidan couldn't live through such a cataclysm again. He wouldn't. He'd been as vulnerable as a newborn pup, no defenses at all.

This time he was smarter.

When he was chilled to the bone, he returned to the bedroom. The small lamp still burned. Emma looked like a painting, her golden hair strewn across the pillow, her ivory breasts rising and falling with each breath.

He climbed beneath the covers, his heart catching sharply in his chest when she murmured and curled into his embrace.

"You're so cold," she said. She didn't open her eyes, but her face scrunched up in dismay.

"Sorry." Her skin felt like velvet—warm, supple and soft.

Even half-asleep, she tried to protect him. She patted his thigh. "Stay close to me." The words were slurred. "I'll warm you up."

For the remainder of the early morning, he listened to her gentle breathing, his body wrapped around hers. It was too important a moment to be lost in sleep. He loved her.

I love you.

No one was there to hear when he whispered the admission, dry-eyed. He loved Emma Braithwaite. Perhaps he had never stopped. But now was all there was. Come daybreak he had to let her go.

Though he closed his eyes, he kept slumber at bay. Around seven-thirty, she stirred. He feigned sleep, giving her the chance to make a trip to the bathroom, to find her clothes and to dress.

When she was ready, he pretended to wake up, rearing up on one elbow to gaze at her sleepily. "You're leaving?"

Emma's smile was shy. "I have to go home and shower and open the shop. Mrs. Correll is coming at two so I can get ready for the wedding, but I'll be on my own until then."

She sat down on the side of the bed and touched his arm. "I wanted to ask you one more thing. If you don't mind."

He tensed inwardly. "What is it?"

Emma glanced down, her expression troubled. When she looked up at him again, he felt as if he could see into her soul. "How long ago was it that Danielle died?" she asked, the words barely audible.

Here it was. This was his chance. All he had to do was tell the truth and he'd be free of Emma forever. She would be hurt, but she deserved to suffer a little. It was only fair.

Feeling cold to his bones, even though the bed still carried the warmth of their two bodies, he looked at her grimly. "Ten years." When the words left his mouth, it was too late to change his mind.

As he watched, Emma's forehead creased. He saw her do the math. "But you left England ten years ago... the first week in December. And you were engaged by Christmas?" Her voice broke on the last word as she stumbled to her feet. "You and Danielle were together before you came to England, weren't you?" Her tone was less accusatory than grief-stricken. She had gone so white, he feared for a moment she would faint.

"I guess you weren't the only one with secrets, Emma. Perhaps no one is ever who they seem."

Sixteen

Emma didn't react outwardly. Not even a single tear. She couldn't. Not with him watching. The hurt ran too deep. It was all she could do to breathe and move one foot in front of the other. She was perfectly calm as she walked out of Aidan's suite and rode the elevator down to the lobby. In the early morning there were few people around other than employees. She was not a hotel guest. Anyone could draw a conclusion from that. But what did it matter?

Perhaps she shouldn't have gotten behind the wheel of a car. But the choking need to put distance between herself and Aidan won out. She kept her speed ten miles under the limit. The mountain road was tricky.

By the time she made it to her apartment, she hovered on the brink of an ugly crying jag. Her chest felt as if someone had ripped it open with a dull blade. Her eyes burned. Her stomach revolted.

Upstairs, she glanced at the clock. In barely an hour she had to open the store for one of the biggest shopping days of the year. What was she going to do? She lay across her bed, utterly lost. Aidan was lying. He had to be. He could never have spent time with her at Oxford, adoring her, having sex with her, making plans with her…if he had been in love with another woman. It was impossible. She refused to believe it.

But then she saw his face as it had been when she walked out of his bedroom. She remembered his dark-eyed stare. And she realized he was right. She didn't know him at all.

Raw, brokenhearted sobs wet her pillow and left her feeling hollow and sick to her stomach. Somehow she had to make it through this day. Somehow she had to survive seeing him one more time. Tonight was Dylan and Mia's wedding. Neither Emma nor Aidan had the luxury of avoiding one another.

Though the thought of it was beyond comprehension, she knew she had no choice. She gave herself twenty minutes to cry out her misery and pain. It wasn't enough. It would never be enough. The empty cavity where her heart normally resided was frightening…like a black hole waiting to swallow her until she was nothing but a spot of darkness.

She dragged herself to her feet and undressed, ashamed that she had no underwear. What had seemed sexy and fun the night before now carried the tawdry feel of regret. A blistering hot shower did nothing to warm her soul. She dried her hair, applied light makeup with trembling hands, and dressed in a wool sweater and pants.

In a very real sense, Silver Memories became her salvation during the day. The heavy flow of customers, the constant *ching* of the cash register…all of it anesthetized her so that she could function.

When Mrs. Correll arrived midafternoon, the older woman didn't appear to notice anything amiss in her boss's demeanor. They exchanged a few words, Emma handed over the keys and fled upstairs.

For the longest time she sat huddled in her chair by

the fire, remembering how Aidan had looked sleeping in this very spot. She wanted to wail and throw things and smash bits of glass, but she was very afraid if she gave in to the emotions tearing her apart, she would never regain control.

The afternoon ticked away until it was far past time to prepare. She forced herself to heat a can of soup and eat it. She had skipped lunch. Though hunger was the last thing on her mind, she knew she needed the sustenance.

At last, she went to her tiny closet and reached for the green velvet dress. It was as beautiful as when she had first opened the box and lifted it out. The style was reminiscent of the 1940s, nipped in at the waist, full-skirted and cut low at the bodice with a sweetheart neckline. Trying it on had made her feel like a movie star.

Now, looking at herself in the mirror, all she saw was the ghost of a woman with sad eyes and a barely beating heart.

The skies had been clear all day, which meant that by five, the temperatures started to plummet. Emma was to be at the church at five thirty for pictures. Although she was only in charge of the guestbook, Mia had insisted she be included.

The small chapel where Mia and Dylan had chosen to have their ceremony was one of the oldest structures in Silver Glen. In lean, hard times, the early townspeople had erected a place of worship, nondenominational, welcoming all who wanted to come.

Only two blocks from Emma's apartment, the historic building was a favorite stop for tourists in the summertime. Tonight, even though Emma walked quickly in her high heels, the wind cut through her thick wool coat as if she were naked.

Breathless when she arrived, she paused at the doors

to the church, drawing on the faith taught to her as a child for strength to face the night ahead. Then lifting her chin, she turned the polished tin knob and let herself in.

The well-worn pews were original wood, as was the floor. Etched windows had been a later addition. Instead of stained glass, they were clear, affording grand views of the mountains in the daytime.

Candles in hurricane globes flickered softly on the high windowsills. Someone, Maeve perhaps, had surrounded them with fresh evergreens and red bows. The scent took Emma back to England, when her rambling, drafty home was decked out in holiday array.

A small group of people milled at the front of the chapel. Mia had refused to give credence to silly superstitions, as she called them, so all the pictures were to be taken with bride and groom together. Dylan couldn't take his eyes off her. His pride and happiness wrapped his woman in a romantic glow. Cora was passed from arm to arm, everyone fighting for the privilege of holding her.

Emma and Aidan stayed on opposite sides of the group, never making eye contact. No one seemed to notice. The photographer was talented and socially adept. He managed to get what he wanted without making anyone feel rushed or stressed. By a quarter 'til seven, it was all done.

Mia disappeared into a small room at the back, where she would wait until it was time for the ceremony. Her parents took a seat on the front row, left-hand side. Four of Mia's friends from Raleigh sat behind them. The Kavanagh boys, resplendent in formal wear, settled beside and behind their mother on the opposite side of the church.

The guest list was relatively small. Over the next half hour, thirty or so people drifted in, all of them longtime friends of the Kavanaghs. Emma offered the book and pen as each couple appeared. Standing so near the door, she shivered, but at least she was as far away from Aidan as possible.

At seven twenty-five, a violinist began to play softly. Emma made sure the old paneled door was firmly latched before taking a seat in the back row. Moments later, the musician began playing an evocative piece that echoed Mia's Russian heritage.

The bride appeared and stood in the center of the aisle. Her eye caught Emma's for a split second. The two women exchanged a smile. Then as the music swelled and danced, Mia walked slowly toward Dylan carrying a bouquet of red roses and eucalyptus tied with gold braid.

Her traditional wedding gown suited her small frame. White satin with long transparent sleeves, the dress's simplicity was a perfect foil for the antique lace that covered the bride's head and reached the floor in back. The veil and pearl-studded headpiece had belonged to Mia's Russian great-grandmother.

The bridal couple had chosen not to have attendants. Only the robed minister stood with them at the chancel rail.

Dearly beloved...

At that moment, Emma lost her composure. Tears rolled, one after the other, down her cheeks. If she had not made such foolish mistakes when she was younger, she and Aidan might have been married a long time by now...perhaps even had children.

Extracting an embroidered handkerchief that had belonged to her grandmother from her clutch purse, she dabbed her cheeks. This was why she felt so much passion for preserving the past. Tangible objects carried the memories of loved ones. They recalled the beauty of earlier times.

Silver Glen had made a point of preserving its heritage, of telling the town's story. And on virtually every street, some evidence of Kavanagh influence could be seen. Aidan was a part of that, though he chose to live elsewhere. Would he ever want to come home for good?

All she could see of him at the moment was the back of his head. She was grateful for that. If he had stood beside his brother, Emma would have been hard-pressed to look away.

She refocused her attention on the minister, who was guiding his charges in repeating wedding vows to each other. Dylan, sensitive to his struggles with the written word, had wanted to use the traditional liturgy. *To have and to hold, in sickness and in health, 'til death do us part.*

The words resonated, beautiful and timeless.

Even in profile, holding hands, Dylan and Mia looked so happy. The tenderness on his face was almost too personal to witness.

When Aidan became part of Emma's life in Oxford, he had looked at her much the same way. She had felt his love to the marrow of her bones. Had never doubted him for a minute. Despite what he told her this morning about the timing of his engagement, she knew he had loved her once upon a time.

Maybe she was blind…or ridiculously naive, but she refused to believe that the Aidan Kavanagh she knew in England was that good an actor.

The minister gave the pronouncement. Dylan and Mia faced their guests, arm in arm, beaming. Someone handed Cora to them. Cheers broke out in the small chapel.

There was no recessional. Everyone stood in the aisle,

talking and laughing. Emma made her way to the front, hugged Dylan and Mia, and prepared to make her escape.

But she hadn't counted on Maeve Kavanagh. Emma was four rows away from the back door and a clean getaway when Aidan's mother hailed her. "Slow down, Emma, for heaven's sake. You don't want to be the first one at the reception."

It didn't seem polite to say that Emma had planned to avoid the post-ceremony soiree all together. "Did I forget something? I put the guestbook in Mia's tote bag like she asked me to…"

Maeve shook her head. "This isn't about the guestbook. I wanted to let you know that I booked a room at the hotel for you tonight."

"Why would you do that? I live here."

"We Kavanaghs know how to throw a party. And though this group tonight will be small, don't underestimate their enthusiasm. We're going to give Dylan and Mia the send-off they deserve. Which means a late night. Grab a toothbrush and whatever else you need and don't argue with the mother of the groom."

"Seriously, Maeve. I'm touched that you want me there, but I don't know any of your guests."

"You know Aidan." Something about the other woman's sly glance told Emma that Maeve was perhaps a bit too perceptive when it came to her sons. "And here he is now."

Emma's stomach flipped hard. Maeve had crooked a finger, and her son, clearly not willing to spoil a family occasion, had come as commanded. But the cold, closed look on his face when he looked at Emma said he was not happy about the situation.

Maeve ignored any tension. "Aidan…I need you to give Emma a ride to her apartment so she can pack a few things. Then bring her up the mountain. I've promised her a room."

"Why?"

Even Maeve faltered at the incredulity in that one syllable. "Well," she said, soldiering on despite the awkward moment, "she will want to have some wine, at least, and no one should drive that mountain road on a dark winter night when she's been drinking."

Aidan shoved the heels of his hands in his eyes. "Mother, you're meddling…and not very subtly. Emma has a perfectly fine vehicle and impeccable driving skills. If she wants to come to the party, she can come on her own."

Maeve bristled. "Watch your tongue, Aidan. You might be a grown man, but you're still my little boy. And I raised you better than that. Apologize to Emma."

Aidan glanced at Emma, his jaw tight. "I'm sorry. I'll be happy to give you a ride up the mountain. Let me get my coat and keys." The bitter sarcasm in his tone was barely veiled, yet Maeve seemed oblivious.

When Aidan strode away, Maeve touched Emma's arm. "Be patient with him, my dear."

"I don't know what you mean." Emma shifted from one foot to the other, uncomfortable and embarrassed.

Maeve shook her head slightly, her eyes filled with a mix of emotions, the clearest of which was determination. "I saw you leave the hotel this morning, Emma."

Bloody hell. "Oh, but I—"

Aidan's mother stopped her with an upheld hand. "It's none of my business. And I don't want or need explanations. But I love my son. And I want to see him happy."

Emma looked toward the front of the church, where Aidan stood talking to James and Conor. She bit her lip.

"I think you've misunderstood. Aidan doesn't have feelings for me. At least not the good kind."

"He's angry with you right now." It wasn't a question.

"Yes, ma'am."

"And you knew each other before you came here."

Emma nodded. She wasn't a very good liar. "We did."

"That's all I need to know. If you have a past with my son, I'm asking you to not give up on whatever this is between you. He can be bullheaded and emotionally distant, but I swear to you that he feels things deeply. Like the silver mines in these hills, sometimes you have to dig through the layers to find what's worth keeping."

Aidan was on his way back down the aisle.

"I understand," Emma whispered. "But there's a lot you don't know."

Maeve patted her arm. "And I don't need to know. Just remember what I said." She touched the skirt of Emma's dress as Aidan joined them. "Doesn't Emma look gorgeous in this shade of green, Aidan?"

"Stop it, Mother."

His parent lifted both eyebrows with an innocent expression. "I don't know what you mean."

"Matchmaking. You're embarrassing Emma."

"Am I?" She looked at Emma beseechingly.

With Aidan standing there like judge and jury, Emma had no choice but to tell the truth. "Yes, ma'am. A little bit."

Maeve waved a hand, dismissing their concerns. "Very well. I'll leave you two alone. But don't be long. We don't want to start the party without you."

Seventeen

Aidan strode around the corner, retrieved his car and turned the heater on full blast as he approached the church and idled at the curb. The door of the old building opened a crack. Emma spotted him and hurried outside, bundled to the chin as she slid into the passenger seat.

"Thank you," she said quietly. "I could have walked back, but I appreciate the lift. It's colder now than it was when I came. And don't worry. I'll drive myself up the mountain."

"Oh, no," he said. "My mother has spoken. My life wouldn't be worth two cents if she found out I didn't follow her directive."

The brief drive was silent after that. Aidan parked in front of Silver Memories. "I'll wait here." He didn't want to see Emma's cozy apartment again. Nor did he want to remember the first time they had made love. Damn his mother for interfering.

He could have told Maeve to go to the devil, but given all that she had sacrificed over the years for Aidan's sorry hide, he didn't have it in him to treat her so shabbily. She was simply trying to help in the only way she knew how.

When Emma reappeared carrying a small suitcase, he hopped out of the car, took it from her and placed it carefully in the trunk. After that, neither of them spoke as they made their way up the winding mountain road. Despite the silence, however, he was stingingly aware of everything about his passenger.

Her scent. Her body language. The way her soft velvet skirt spread across the seat, nearly touching his thigh.

This morning he had been so sure about everything. But tonight, seated in a hundred-year-old church, watching his brother marry the love of his life amidst the romantic glow of candlelight, even Aidan's calcified heart had begun to quiver and crack.

When all was said and done, did it matter that Emma had betrayed him once upon a time? Could he put the past behind him?

His introspection was short-lived. Soon, the magnificent hotel, ablaze with lights, welcomed them. Though all the family benefitted materially from the hotel's success, Liam and Maeve were the forces behind the day-to-day operations.

As Aidan exited the car and handed over the keys, Emma walked on ahead of him. To any onlooker, it might have seemed as if she were trying to get in out of the cold. But Aidan knew the truth. She didn't want him to touch her…even something as innocuous as holding her elbow as they ascended the steps.

The elegant lobby was festive and crowded. The long-time concierge, Pierre, directed them to a private room at the back of the hotel. Aidan and Emma were the last to arrive. Only Cora was missing. Dylan's housekeeper had taken the baby home to put her to bed.

Aidan grabbed a beer and some food and made a bee-line for an unoccupied seat near Gavin. His brother shot him a look rife with curiosity. "You not hanging with your girlfriend?"

Stabbing a canapé with a silver fork, Aidan shook his head. "Not my girlfriend."

"Mom seems to think differently."

"Mom is a busybody."

Maeve appeared out of nowhere to thump him on the back of his head. "I heard that."

Aidan gave her a measured look. "If the shoe fits…"

She bent to kiss his cheek. "My job is to see my children settled happily."

Gavin blanched. "Don't get any ideas about me. Two out of seven isn't bad, Mom."

"Don't worry," she said. "When the right woman comes along, I won't have to do a thing. I love seeing my big strong boys give in to love." She didn't pause to sit down. "Pay attention now. Mia and Dylan are about to cut the cake."

Aidan turned his gaze to the appropriate spot in the room, but he couldn't help tracking Emma. So far tonight, she had been introduced to Mia's Raleigh friends, and she had danced with at least three of Aidan's brothers, including the groom.

As far as he could tell, she was having a wonderful time.

The more Emma glowed, the more Aidan glowered. He'd told her today that he had lied to her and cheated on her. Did she not believe him? Or did his confession not matter at all?

He couldn't understand her. That infuriated him more than anything. He was accustomed to sizing up a man or a woman at first meeting. Such people skills made him successful in his work.

But Emma remained an enigma. When he was in bed with her, it was easy to pretend she was the girl he knew in England, the young woman who made his life complete.

With a bit of emotional distance, though, his cynicism returned in full force. People didn't change. If Emma had betrayed him before, it was in her DNA to do it again. No matter how good the sex—and even he would admit that it was pretty damn spectacular—he would be a fool to set himself up for disappointment and loss a second time.

It was bad enough that he loved her. But he would get over that. He had to. He also had to make it clear to her and to himself that whatever her reasons for coming to Silver Glen…he wasn't interested.

The hours passed slowly. Never once did Emma glance his way. In her deep emerald pin-up-girl dress, she laughed and chatted and danced and partied the night away. He studied her for long chunks of time, trying to decide what it was about her that called to him. Was it the classic features? The golden hair? The female chuckle that went straight to his gut and ignited a slow burn? Seeing Conor pull her out onto the floor a second time made Aidan clench his jaw. But he kept his seat.

Emma could dance with every man in Silver Glen for all he cared.

Only for Mia did Aidan make an exception. His new sister-in-law sparkled with happiness. "I've danced with everyone but you," she said, taking him by the hand and pulling him to his feet. "You're acting like Scrooge over here in your corner. Don't make me beg."

"I wouldn't dream of it," he said, smiling at her with affection. "You've made my brother a very happy man."

Mia returned the smile. "Your whole family has welcomed me so sweetly. It's a novelty to have brothers after all this time. But I think I like it." He steered her around the floor, responding to her happy chatter when appropriate. Mia was an exceptional woman in every way. But never once had he felt anything for her other than fondness and admiration.

Even if Dylan hadn't been in the picture, Aidan wouldn't have made a play for Mia. Because no matter how foolish and self-destructive it was, the only female who gave him sleepless nights and unfulfilled sexual dreams was Emma Braithwaite.

At the song's end, he delivered Mia back to her new groom. Then, trying not to be obvious about it, he scouted the room for Emma's location. She was nowhere to be seen.

He couldn't ask about her, or he'd risk setting off his mother's radar. After half an hour, when it was clear Emma hadn't merely slipped out to the restroom, Aidan gave the bridal couple and his mother one last set of hugs and said his goodbyes. If they were suspicious, they gave no sign.

In the lobby, he hesitated. Everyone on staff knew him. It wasn't as if he could make an inquiry on the sly. So he might as well sin and sin boldly.

He approached the check-in area, giving Marjorie, the desk clerk who had known him since he was a boy, his best winsome smile.

Lowering his voice, he leaned an elbow on the granite counter. "Can you please give me Emma Braithwaite's room number? She slipped out before I had a chance to tell her good-night."

Marjorie eyed him with a wry twist of her lips. "Is this going to get me in trouble, Aidan?"

He held up his hands. "Not at all. I swear."

Shaking her head, she jotted the number on a slip of paper and pushed it toward him. "Don't make me regret this."

"I'm on my best behavior."

She snorted. "When it comes to Kavanagh men, that definition has all sorts of interpretations. Good luck."

"With what?" He lifted an eyebrow.

"The pretty English lady. You could do a lot worse."

"Forget that," he chuckled, though his throat was tight. "I haven't caught wedding fever, despite all the festivities. This confirmed bachelor is completely content with his lot."

Emma unpinned her hair and brushed it out. After taking off her stockings and shoes, she curled up on the sofa. Though this room was nowhere near as large as Aidan's suite, it was nevertheless extremely luxurious. More for company than anything else, she turned on the television and muted it.

Two different channels were showing the classic holiday movie *White Christmas*. She paused on one, but it was late in the film. Rosemary Clooney and Bing Crosby had argued and were in the midst of a party, trying to ignore each other. The similarities between the fictional couple and Aidan and Emma were hard to miss.

Even Rosemary's clothing struck a chord, perhaps the reason Emma had ordered this particular style and color for Mia's wedding. She couldn't bring herself to take off the dress yet. The soft green velvet buoyed her spirits and made her feel feminine, despite her sad mood.

When the knock sounded at her door, she couldn't even say she was surprised. But her heart skipped a few beats anyway.

After glancing through the peephole, she unlocked the dead bolt and opened it. Aidan lingered in the hallway, his expression hard to read.

"May I come in?" he asked, his formal tone at odds with the turbulence in his gaze.

"Of course." She stepped back to allow him to enter.

He prowled the confines of her room, hands shoved in his pockets. "I thought you would be angry," he said.

"About what?"

"Don't play dumb. About what I told you this morning. The timing of my engagement."

She debated how to answer him. "We both made mistakes, Aidan. I'm hardly one to criticize."

"Are you even human?" he snapped. "Why aren't you calling me names? Why aren't you throwing things at me?"

"For the same reason that you're in my room right now," she said quietly, her heart breaking. "We don't know how to be together because we ruined the past, but there's something between us that we haven't managed to kill."

He ripped off his tie and ran a hand behind his neck. "I'm leaving in the morning." The dark-eyed gaze dared her to protest.

Emma shook her head vehemently. "Your mother will be crushed, Aidan. She's so looking forward to having her whole family together on Christmas Day. And the special events this week, the children's party, the caroling—please don't leave. I'll go instead. You won't have to see me again."

"Where would you go?"

"Back to England, I suppose."

"But your mother is traveling. That's why Mia and my mom have included you as part of our family this past week."

"It doesn't matter. I'm not a Kavanagh. But you *are*, Aidan. You can't forsake your family this year. If you do, they'll realize that you've never gotten over losing Danielle. And somehow, I think you don't want them to know that."

"What makes you think I've never gotten over Danielle?" Hostility crackled in the words.

"I heard it in your voice this morning. You loved her. And you lost her in a tragic accident. Being here in Silver Glen at Christmas has revived those terrible memories."

Aidan felt as if were being ripped apart. He knew exactly what kind of ass he would be to abandon his family now. But God knows, it seemed like his only choice at the moment.

Allowing Emma to leave Silver Glen would accomplish nothing. He was deliberately fostering the lie that Danielle was his long-lost love…that he had kept an emotional vigil for her all these years.

If that lie was supposed to be a punishment for Emma, then why was *he* the one who felt like hell?

"I can't stay," he said bluntly. "I don't want to."

Emma wrung her hands. "But you have to," she cried. In her bare feet, and with her hair loose around her face, she looked more like the girl he had loved in Oxford.

"Perhaps you could convince me," he said slowly. *Bastard*. His mind was made up, and yet he was willing to use Emma's concern as a bargaining chip. In his defense, if he were never going to see her again, surely it wasn't such a terrible crime to steal one more night in her arms.

She stared at him in silence. Even disheveled and upset, her dignity was unassailable. Inevitably, he felt like a peasant begging for crumbs.

"Say something," he growled. "Yes or no?"

He watched her chest rise and fall. Blue eyes, tinged

with some painful emotion, judged him and found him wanting.

"Yes."

The exultation that swept through his veins was at odds with Emma's expression. Her misery infuriated him. "You don't have to look like a condemned woman on her way to the guillotine. If you don't want me, say so. I'm done playing games."

Her quiet laugh held no amusement at all. "It's not a game, Aidan, believe me."

When she turned on her heel and left him standing alone in the sitting area, he gaped. The bathroom door opened and closed. He heard water running.

Grim-faced, he pounded on the wood. "Quit hiding from me, damn it. And don't undress. That's my job."

She swung open the barrier between them so quickly he almost pitched forward. Her eyes flashed blue fire. "Fine. Have it your way." She stalked toward the bed and stood beside it, her back to him. She had swept her hair over one shoulder, baring the nape of her neck.

A pulse, low and sweet, began to thrum in his veins. He closed the distance between them. "I'm not a big fan of angry sex," he whispered, kissing the top of her spine. "Let's forget everything tonight except for the way we make each other feel."

Glancing at him over her shoulder, she gave him a mocking smile. "You mean the way we want to strangle each other?"

Eighteen

How could she make him want to laugh at the oddest moments? He shook his head. "I don't want to strangle you, Emma. At least not most of the time." He was forced to add that last bit in the interest of honesty.

She sighed and bowed her head, her posture submissive despite her sarcasm. "We seem to make better enemies than we do friends."

The phrasing bothered him. "I don't want to be your friend." These feelings he had were too strong for friendship and too complicated for anything else.

When she turned to face him, he held her by the shoulders...suddenly afraid she would bolt.

Emma was smaller and more vulnerable in her bare feet. She tilted her face up to his and studied him intently, as if trying to see inside his soul. "We were friends once upon a time."

"No." He shook his head, the word vehement. "We were lovers. I never had time to be your friend, because the first day I met you I fell head over heels in lust with you."

"Lust? Not love?"

He had no doubt he was hurting her now. "Lust, Emma," he said flatly, "a young man's physical passion for a beautiful woman. Love lasts. Lust fades. That's how you know the difference. If we ever had a shot at love, it ended before it began."

"And yet you still want me."

Only then did he see the trap he had set for himself. *Damn.* He backtracked quickly. "But only because we've been thrown together in this Christmas-wedding, romantic atmosphere. It's not real. *We're* not real. I wasn't kidding when I said I'm leaving in the morning. And no matter what I intimated, you can't change my mind."

Her small smile was wistful. "Final answer?"

He steeled himself against her charm. "Final answer. Now, do you want me under those conditions, or not?"

Two soft hands cupped his face. Feminine fingers slid cool against his overheated skin. Her eyes searched his. "I love you, Aidan. I know you'd rather not hear it. Perhaps you don't believe it. Or maybe our history discredits what I say. But before you leave, I want you to understand how I feel. I don't know what Danielle has to do with all of this, but she's gone and I'm here. I can't change what happened in England. I'm sorry for that. But please, Aidan. Don't live in the past."

Every word she spoke was a shard of glass, piercing his skin and finding its way to his heart. *Emma loved him.* He wanted to crow with masculine triumph. Beat his chest. Shout it from the rooftops.

Yet in the midst of all that rose a terrible pain. He'd believed her once upon a time. Had handed over his heart with the carelessness of youth, not realizing what he risked.

Three times he'd been betrayed by love. His father had not loved his sons enough to put them before his obsession with finding a lost silver mine. Danielle had died, leaving Aidan with the guilt of knowing he hadn't loved her enough. And Emma…Emma had made him *believe* in love. That was the cruelest blow of all.

His heart encased in ice, he removed her hands from his face and forced her arms behind her back, manacling her wrists with one hand. Her bones, delicate in his grasp, struck him as feminine and helpless. "I don't want you to love me," he said. He crushed his mouth over hers taking the kiss he wanted, feeling the way her lips quivered against his. "All I want is you."

Emma felt the sting of hot tears and blinked them back. She had gambled her all on one roll of the dice and lost. Gasping, she struggled to free her arms. "I want you, too," she whispered. "But I don't like angry sex, either. Come to bed with me, Aidan."

He let her go instantly and stood stone faced as she reached behind her to lower the zipper. When she faltered, he finished the task, holding her hand as she stepped out of a sea of velvet. Carefully, he draped the dress over a nearby chair.

She saw Aidan's eyes burn as he took in the matching bra, undies and garter belt she wore. Her nipples tightened in helpless pleasure. His hot gaze raked her from head to toe, leaving no doubt about his desire for her. A less pragmatic woman might have told herself that love was there buried somewhere under that brusque facade.

But she had come too far to fool herself now. Aidan wanted her body—not her soul, not her heart, not her whispered confession of devotion. And because she loved him enough for two, she would give him everything. If that left her with nothing, she would not cry.

Taking his hand, she climbed into the bed. He was on her instantly, his face flushed, the bulge in his trousers impossible to miss. They kissed wildly. He tasted of coffee and wedding cake.

"God, you drive me insane," he muttered, sucking one nipple through a covering of ecru lace. "Tell me you want me."

She unbuttoned his shirt with fumbling fingers. "I do, Aidan. I do."

The juxtaposition of those five words so close to tonight's wedding ceremony made him wince. Emma saw his involuntary response. Though she hadn't meant to make the connection—obviously, he had.

He rolled away from her long enough to toe off his shoes and unfasten his trousers. When he freed his sex, it was dark red and rigid. "Can't wait," he groaned. "Not this time."

The fact that he didn't bother to finish undressing either of them was as arousing as the touch of his big warm hands on her body. "Then don't," she said, tugging him closer.

He took two seconds to move aside the narrow fabric between her legs. Then he positioned himself and shoved to the hilt in one forceful thrust that smacked the headboard against the wall.

A ragged laugh shook his chest. "Please tell me I didn't bust a hole in the wall. I'd never live it down."

"Do you really care?" She linked her ankles at the small of his back. Neither of them was naked. Yet this was the most intimate time she had shared with him since he'd arrived in Silver Glen.

For a flash—a split second—he looked down at her with the face of the young man who had stolen her heart. Carefree. Happy. Determined to make her his. "No. I suppose not," he muttered.

Keeping his gaze locked on her face, he moved inside her. One steady push after another. His skin heated. So did hers. The pace was lazy, but the look in his eyes was anything but.

"Tell me what you're thinking," she said, the words tumbling out impulsively.

It was a mistake. Instantly, his expression shuttered. His jaw rigid, he closed his eyes and closed her out.

Beneath her fingertips, his hair was soft and springy. Her thighs ached from the effort of clinging to him. He overwhelmed her suddenly, so much a man that she could almost forget the boy.

But even as he stroked her intimately, she felt echoes of sweetness from the past. Almost everything had changed. The world. Their lives. Their bodies. Yet when she closed her eyes and gave herself over to the intense pleasure of the moment, she could pretend she was back in England. Back with a young Aidan. Back under the influence of a love that was innocent and perfect.

Without warning, he shifted suddenly, putting pressure where her body craved his touch. She shivered, so close to her climax that she felt little flutters of anticipation in her sex.

Aidan nipped her earlobe with sharp teeth. "I'll stay 'til morning." The promise was hoarse.

"Yes." It was all she could manage. He took her with him then to a place that held a poignant mixture of regret and physical bliss.

"Emma…"

She couldn't answer him in words. Her throat was too tight. Instead, she rained kisses across his face and canted her hips to take him deeper. He groaned as if he were in pain when he came. And she followed him. But the pleasure was hollow and the end incomplete.

Because what he gave her was not enough. And it never would be.

Nineteen

Aidan huddled into his wool overcoat, turning up the collar in a vain attempt to escape the howling wind from the arctic front that had blasted through New York that morning. Snow fell, but it was dry and icy…nothing to hamper shoppers on the next-to-last shopping day before Christmas.

He'd been walking the streets of Manhattan for hours, his hands and his feet numb. The physical discomfort was some kind of punishment, though he didn't know exactly what for or why. All he knew was that he'd been compelled to leave his apartment in search of relief from his pain.

Booze hadn't done it. Nor back-to-back movies at the closest theater. Not even an impulsive volunteer shift at a local soup kitchen…though that last stint had at least reminded him that holiday misery took on a far more serious face in many corners and back alleys of the city.

Everywhere he went he faced incessant, relentless good cheer. Even the poor and downtrodden found something to smile about in the presence of an artificial tree and modest gifts from local charities.

Aidan was so lost he couldn't even begin to find the path. The life he'd been so pleased with before he decided to spend Christmas at Silver Glen was gone, eradicated by the memories of Emma.

He saw her in every window display, in every shiny package carried by smiling passersby. Everything good and joyful and meaningful about Christmas conspired to remind him that true love meant forgiveness. It was that simple. And that impossible.

He could forgive Emma for just about anything, if the truth were told. But what if he had her and lost her again?

Imagining such a thing made him shudder with a biting chill that was far worse than any winter weather he could conjure. He wanted his old life back…the one where he didn't *have* to feel anything. A satisfying job. A pleasant social life. And plenty of his own company.

Where was *that* Aidan Kavanagh?

At last, when his face was in danger of frostbite, he headed for home. Leftover pizza in the fridge would be his companion tonight. Hopefully, none of his family would ring him up again. He'd already fielded one tearful phone call from his mother that left him feeling like the worst kind of vermin on the planet.

Hell, Dylan had even texted Aidan from his honeymoon and called him a handful of choice names that were spot on. Without even trying, Aidan had become something worse than a Scrooge…if there was such a thing.

When he reached his building, he gave the doorman a fifty-dollar tip and a muttered "Merry Christmas." But he never made it to his apartment. When he stepped off the elevator, Mr. Shapiro, his across-the-hall neighbor, appeared, wild-eyed.

"Help me, Aidan," he cried. "Mrs. S. fell in the kitchen and she's out cold."

Aidan dashed into the apartment with him. "Have you called 911?"

The old man wrung his hands. "Yes. But how long will it take?"

As Aidan knelt beside the white-haired lady, he thought he heard sirens in the distance. "Hang on, Mr. Shapiro. She's breathing." That was a relief. Surely things couldn't be too bad. Had she passed out and fallen, or had she fallen and passed out after she hit her head? "Grab me a pillow and something to cover her with. We don't want her to get cold here on the floor."

Aidan was not a trained medic, but even he could see that the poor guy needed something to do.

Fortunately, the EMTs made it upstairs in the next ten minutes. They loaded the elderly woman onto a gurney and rolled her out into the hall. Mr. Shapiro looked pale enough to pass out himself.

A uniformed kid who looked all of twenty smiled encouragingly. "We're taking her to Lenox Hospital. Don't worry. She seems to be stable."

Suddenly, the professionals were gone. Mr. Shapiro seemed at a loss. He had to be ninety if he were a day. And the poor guy was shaking all over. "Let me get you something to drink," Aidan said. "I think you need to sit down."

Suddenly the man's spine snapped straight. "I'm fine. Take me to see her. Please?"

The naked entreaty in his wrinkled face was impossible to resist, even if Aidan had possessed a heart of stone. "Of course." Aidan pulled out his phone and summoned a cab. When he turned around, Mr. Shapiro was standing in front of a menorah, his lips moving in a quiet prayer.

"Are you ready?" Aidan asked quietly.

The man nodded, plucking his jacket from an antique coat tree. "What should I take for her?" he asked suddenly, the agitation returning to his face.

"If she needs anything later, I'll bring you back here," Aidan promised.

Aidan's apartment was only three blocks from the hospital, but the old man was in no condition to walk, especially not on a night that was as wickedly cold as this one.

The cab ride took no time at all. Aidan paid the fare and jumped out to help Mr. Shapiro. They didn't need a broken bone to add to the evening's trauma.

Inside the hospital, the emergency room admitting nurse was kind but firm. "No one can go back yet. Give them time to assess her condition and make sure she's stable. I'll keep you posted."

Aidan found a couple of chairs, and the two of them sat down. Moments later, Mr. Shapiro's chin rested on his chest. He was either sleeping or praying again.

When he lifted his head and spoke suddenly, it startled Aidan. His gaze was clear and sharp in a face that was worn with time. "We've been married seventy-one years. Came over during the Second World War as newlyweds. Our families pooled money for our passage. We lost them all in the holocaust. Esther is all I have in the world."

"No children?" Aidan asked quietly.

"We couldn't have any."

The silence lengthened after that. Aidan felt the story in his bones. Love and loss. The fabric of life.

At last, when the summons came, Mr. Shapiro jumped to his feet like a young lad.

Aidan touched his arm. "Do you want me to go back with you?"

"I'd like that. You're a good boy."

It had been many years since Aidan had considered himself a boy, but from Mr. Shapiro's perspective, the reference made sense.

They made their way back to a tiny exam room. "I'll

stay in the hall for now," Aidan said. "You tell me if you need me."

The door was open and stayed open, so Aidan hovered just out of sight. When he took a quick peek, he saw Mrs. Shapiro's arms go up to embrace her husband. The look on the old woman's face made something hurt in Aidan's chest. The moment was intensely personal, yet he couldn't look away. For a split second he could see the couple as twenty-somethings, walking the streets of New York arm in arm.

Forcing himself to back up, he leaned against the wall in the corridor and shut his eyes. Five minutes passed, maybe ten, before Mr. Shapiro touched his arm. Though stooped and shuffling, the devoted husband smiled with relief. "It was a mild heart attack," he said. "But she's going to be okay. They're keeping her overnight. She wants me to go home and get some rest."

Aidan nodded. "Sounds good."

In Mr. Shapiro's apartment, Aidan prepared to say his goodbyes. But his neighbor sank into a chair, his gnarled hands gripping the arms white-knuckled. "I'll sit here tonight," he said.

"Why on earth would you do that?"

Mr. Shapiro grimaced. "My hearing's gone. I don't want to miss the phone if the hospital calls. She might need me."

"What if I sleep on your sofa?" Aidan said. "You need to keep up your strength so you can take care of your wife. If the hospital contacts you, I'll make sure to wake you up."

The old man sniffed and wiped his nose with the back of his hand. His rheumy eyes held a wealth of gratitude. "God bless you, Mr. Kavanagh."

"Call me Aidan…please."

"And I'm Howard."

The two men stared at each other, opposites in every way. One young, one old. Two different faiths. One with more family than he knew what to do with. The other alone in the world.

Aidan knew in that moment that something had changed. No longer would he be able to hide behind the anonymity of the city. From the first moment he set eyes on Emma again and realized he still wanted her, the painful process of metamorphosis had begun. The man he had been was gone. But who would surface in his place?

Twenty

Emma locked the door to Silver Memories at four o'clock and pulled the shade over the glass. Fastened to the other side was a notice that said: Closed until January 3rd. It had been a good holiday season for her fledgling business. Though financially it wouldn't have mattered one way or another, she took quiet pride in knowing she had pulled it off.

It was Christmas Eve. Maeve had offered numerous invitations to join the Kavanagh clan for the evening and the next day, but Emma declined them all. Holidays were a family time. If that weren't reason enough, Emma bore the guilt of feeling responsible for Aidan's absence.

Maeve hadn't said much on that subject, but Emma knew the Kavanagh matriarch was deeply disappointed not to have her whole clan together. Dylan and Mia had chosen to take a brief honeymoon with a longer trip planned for later. They had returned midday today and were looking forward to spending Christmas Eve with their daughter and the rest of the family.

Mia hadn't called Emma this afternoon. But she was undoubtedly busy. Perhaps she, too, blamed Emma for Aidan's return to New York. Unless Aidan had made any explanations—and that didn't sound like him at all—none of the Kavanaghs could know for sure what was going on. If, however, Maeve had shared what she knew about seeing Emma at the hotel in the early morning hours, then speculation might have filled in the details.

When the shop was set to rights and the till counted, Emma grabbed her coat and the day's deposit in hopes of making a dash to the bank before it closed. The weather was far balmier today than it had been a week ago. She didn't even need gloves or a hat.

People on the street bustled happily. Some of the die-hard shoppers made last-minute purchases, though like Emma, most business owners were closing up for the long weekend.

With her errand done, Emma found herself walking aimlessly, enjoying the waning sunshine and the scent of wood smoke and evergreen in the air. Even though she felt very much alone, she drew comfort from the cheerful "busy"-ness of small-town life.

She recognized many faces now that she had been around for a few months. Silver Glen was a close-knit community and would be a wonderful spot to put down permanent roots. Emma's mother was already talking about coming over for a visit in the New Year.

And as for Aidan…well, that situation would resolve itself. He didn't come home to visit very often, and when he did, Emma planned to make herself scarce.

Without conscious thought, she found herself in front of the chapel where Dylan and Mia had exchanged vows. The town council had decided long ago to leave the little church unlocked at all times, not only for tourists' benefit, but so that the people of Silver Glen could also stop by and say a prayer or light a candle.

Emma opened the door and closed it behind her. It was cold inside the small sanctuary. With the sun going down, shadows spread long and dark across the wooden pews.

In one corner, a simply decorated tree stood ready for the late night service. Candles burned on the altar already. The evergreen boughs from the wedding still adorned the windows.

She sat down on the second row and ran her hand over the velvet cushion. Several generations of Silver Glen's families had worshipped here. Emma felt an unseen connection to the little abbey back home in the Cotswolds.

Breathing slowly, she took stock of her disappointment and grief. Aidan was not hers. He didn't want anything *from* her. She had been so sure she could convince him they deserved a second chance. But in the end, she was forced to recognize the futility of her hopes and dreams.

Whatever Aidan had felt for her once upon a time didn't matter. All that was important now was for Emma to move on.

Even with all that grown-up reasoning, surely a girl deserved a moment to indulge in self-pity. Resting her arms on the pew in front of her, she buried her face and let the tears fall.

But her catharsis was short.

"Emma..."

When a voice sounded behind her, she jerked upright and wiped her cheeks with trembling fingers before turning around. The shadows were deeper now. Even so, she recognized the figure standing tall and still in the center aisle.

"Aidan?"

"Yep."

He sounded resigned. Or mildly amused. Or maybe both.

"What are you doing here?"

"Here, where? In Silver Glen? Or in this church?"

"Either. Both." She felt dizzy—hot one minute and cold the next.

"It's Christmas Eve."

He said it calmly as if it were perfectly normal for him to be in the one place that held so many dark memories.

When he took two steps in her direction, she held up both hands. "Stop. Don't come any closer."

He obeyed, but he cocked his head. "Are you scared of me, Emma?" Now, he was near enough for the candles on the altar to illuminate his face. In his dear, familiar features she saw fatigue…but something else as well. Light. Steadiness. Contentment. As if someone had wiped away his customary air of cynicism.

"Please don't say whatever you're going to say," she cried. "I can't bear it. I've made my peace with this whole mess. I need you to go away." Ruthlessly, she stomped on the hope that tried to gain a tiny foothold in the hushed atmosphere.

"I can't, Emma. I owe you an apology and an explanation."

"I don't want it. It's too late. Your family is waiting for you up on the mountain. Go."

He took two more steps, his posture confident and relaxed. "I've made you miserable, Emma. I'm so sorry."

Literally backed into a corner because of the closed-in pew, she inhaled sharply. "I need you to respect my wishes." Unfortunately, the words came out quavering and tearful instead of firm and demanding.

Aidan must have made his own interpretation. He crowded her, his scent and the warmth of his body making her pulse jump. "I love you, Emma."

She put her hands over her ears. "No. Don't say things you think I want to hear. You're in a sacred place. Lightning will strike."

He ran his hands down her arms and tugged her by the wrists until she landed firmly against his chest. One of his thighs lodged between hers. His gray sweater was soft against her cheek. If she listened hard enough, she could hear his heart beating in time with hers.

"Neither of us can dance around the facts beneath this roof, can we? It has to be the truth and nothing but the truth." He stroked her hair. "Sit down with me, Emma."

He didn't give her much choice. Tucking her in the crook of the arm, he cuddled her close.

But she couldn't bear it. Jerking away and standing abruptly, she kept him at bay. "Let me out."

"No."

Emma started to shake. "We've come to the end of the road, Aidan. Don't make things worse."

"I was a free agent when I came to England," he said. "Danielle and I had been dating for a long time. But we weren't sure if what we had was merely comfortable. The decision was mutual. We agreed to see other people while I was gone."

"And at Christmas, you went home and realized that you had loved her all along." It seemed petty and wrong to be jealous of a dead woman, but however unpleasant, the reality was clear.

Their intense conversation was interrupted momentarily when the minister came in and turned on the lights. He halted abruptly when he saw them. "Sorry to interrupt. Just getting ready for tonight. Merry Christmas." He departed as quickly as he had come.

The fixtures were original to the building and could only handle low-wattage bulbs, so even now the room was softly lit. Emma wasn't sure if it were better or worse that she could see Aidan's face more clearly. He remained seated, but she sensed his determination.

"When I left England," he said, "I was a mess. But I was a guy, so I wasn't about to let anyone know how I felt."

"I called you and sent emails for weeks, but you didn't answer."

"In case you haven't noticed, I'm a stubborn man. Even worse, back then I was too young to know that few situations in life are entirely black or white. You had betrayed me. That was all I knew. I got back to campus and saw Danielle. She represented everything uncomplicated and easy. Without thinking about the consequences, I proposed."

"And she accepted."

"Yes. It was something we had thought about for a long time, so the proposal was almost anticlimactic. We made plans to go to Silver Glen and spend Christmas with my family. But by the time we made it to North Carolina, I realized I had made a mistake."

"What kind of mistake?"

"I *loved* her, but I wasn't *in* love with her. I knew I couldn't drag things out, so as soon as the holidays were over, I planned to tell her the truth and to apologize."

"But she died."

After all this time, his face reflected a pain that was still deep. "I failed her on so many levels."

"But you made her happy, too."

"God, I hope so." He raked his hands through his hair, leaning forward with his elbows on his knees. "As soon as I broke things off with Danielle, I planned to go back to England and confront you…to fight for what we had."

"But you didn't…"

"I couldn't." He sat back against the pew, his expression bleak as he stared at her. "How was it fair for me to reach for happiness when her life was over?"

Hearing that Aidan had wanted to come back to England healed some of the raw places in Emma's heart. "I'm so sorry."

He shrugged. "It all happened a long time ago."

"Is it my turn now?" she asked quietly. "Will you let me tell you my story?"

He stood up and took her in his arms a second time, smoothing the hair from her face. "It doesn't matter, Emma. Whatever mistakes you made back then were no better or worse than mine. It's over." She saw the love in his eyes, but she couldn't let him believe that she had betrayed him.

It was her turn to pull him down onto the pew. She half turned to face him, taking his hands in hers. "Richard lied to you."

Aidan frowned. "He introduced himself to me as your fiancé. And when I looked at you to ask if it was true, you hesitated. I saw in your face that you knew who he was and you weren't surprised."

"I wasn't surprised, because my father had been telling Richard for two years that if he only waited for me to finish college, my father was sure that I would consent to an engagement."

"And would you have? Had it not been for me?"

"No," she said firmly. "I'd made that clear to my father, but Richard's estate adjoined ours, and my father had visions of joining two great families, even though Richard was a decade older than I was. Poor Richard was not a malicious man, but he let himself be manipulated by my father. When Daddy got wind of my romance with you, he sent Richard to London to stake a claim."

Aidan closed his eyes momentarily as a pained look crossed his face. "So none of it was true…"

"No. But I handled things poorly. When you asked me

if Richard was my fiancé, I should have denied it immediately. I'd been brought up to keep the peace whenever possible, though. I didn't want to hurt Richard's feelings, because he hadn't really done anything wrong except for letting my father fill his head with nonsense. But in my naïveté, I hurt the one person I loved more than anything else in the world."

"Was that incident what caused the rift with your father?"

"Yes. I was furious and distraught and completely at a loss as to what to do. He ruined my life."

"Or maybe you and I ruined our lives together."

She grimaced, nodding. "A decade lost."

Aidan cupped her face in his hands. "That decade taught me some important lessons, my love. I've come to understand that forgiveness has to be unconditional. And it's finally been pounded into my hard skull that the people who love me don't deserve to be shut out…that our connection and commitment to one another make life rich." He paused, his throat working. "I won't ever let you go again."

Emma trembled, afraid to assume too much. "Meaning what, Aidan?"

He kissed her softly on the lips, a reverent, sweet caress. When he pulled back, his eyes gleamed. "It means that you're going to marry me. The sooner, the better. My work, your antique business—we can handle those details as we go along."

Joy welled in her chest. "Don't I get a say in the matter?"

"Not at all. This is nonnegotiable. But I think we'd better get out of here quickly."

"Why?"

"Because the thoughts I'm having about you right now are definitely not appropriate in this setting."

Outside, he took her in his arms again, and kissing her deeply, backed her up against the door of the church and sealed his vow. He had come so close to losing her a second time, it terrified him. "I love you, Em. Body and soul. I never stopped. I've lied to myself for years, living on the surface of life, never willing to admit that there was more."

Her smile was radiant, warming him even as the chill of night swirled around him. "You're the best Christmas present I've ever received. I love you, too, Aidan. My apartment is close. What if we go there and I show you exactly how much?"

He shuddered, already imagining the feel of her body pressed against his. "Hold that thought, my little tease. There's one thing we have to do first."

Her eyes widened in comprehension. "Of course…"

The Silver Beeches Lodge was booked to capacity. Aidan held Emma's hand as they walked up the steps. As the doorman welcomed then into the lobby, Emma hung back.

"I'm nervous," she whispered.

"Why, my love? You've already met everyone."

"But it's Christmas. And I'm the reason you almost missed it."

"You're also the reason I came back."

Emma's brow furrowed as they headed back toward the small dining room that had been set aside for the Kavanagh celebration. "I forgot to ask. Did you have some kind of epiphany about us?"

He stood in the doorway, his arm around her waist

and surveyed his loud, wonderful family before they had a chance to notice him. The remnants of dinner littered the large table. In the far corner, a mountain of brightly wrapped gifts waited to be opened.

Pressing a kiss to the top of Emma's head, Aidan paused to savor the incredible feeling of happiness and joy that swept over him. "Let's just say that I did the math, and I realized if we start right now, we can still make it to our fiftieth wedding anniversary."

Emma leaned into him, the woman he'd always loved and needed. "Merry Christmas, Aidan," she said.

"Merry Christmas, my English rose..."

* * * * *

*If you loved this novel, don't miss
Liam and Dylan Kavanagh's stories,*

*A NOT-SO-INNOCENT SEDUCTION
BABY FOR KEEPS*

Available now!

*Only from USA TODAY bestselling author
Janice Maynard
and Harlequin Desire!*

REQUEST YOUR FREE BOOKS!
2 FREE NOVELS PLUS 2 FREE GIFTS!

H HARLEQUIN®

Desire

ALWAYS POWERFUL, PASSIONATE AND PROVOCATIVE

YES! Please send me 2 FREE Harlequin Desire® novels and my 2 FREE gifts (gifts are worth about $10). After receiving them, if I don't wish to receive any more books, I can return the shipping statement marked "cancel." If I don't cancel, I will receive 6 brand-new novels every month and be billed just $4.55 per book in the U.S. or $4.99 per book in Canada. That's a savings of at least 13% off the cover price! It's quite a bargain! Shipping and handling is just 50¢ per book in the U.S. and 75¢ per book in Canada.* I understand that accepting the 2 free books and gifts places me under no obligation to buy anything. I can always return a shipment and cancel at any time. Even if I never buy another book, the two free books and gifts are mine to keep forever.

225/326 HDN F4ZC

Name _____ (PLEASE PRINT) _____

Address _____ Apt. # _____

City _____ State/Prov. _____ Zip/Postal Code _____

Signature (if under 18, a parent or guardian must sign)

Mail to the Harlequin® Reader Service:
IN U.S.A.: P.O. Box 1867, Buffalo, NY 14240-1867
IN CANADA: P.O. Box 609, Fort Erie, Ontario L2A 5X3

Want to try two free books from another line?
Call 1-800-873-8635 or visit www.ReaderService.com.

* Terms and prices subject to change without notice. Prices do not include applicable taxes. Sales tax applicable in N.Y. Canadian residents will be charged applicable taxes. Offer not valid in Quebec. This offer is limited to one order per household. Not valid for current subscribers to Harlequin Desire books. All orders subject to credit approval. Credit or debit balances in a customer's account(s) may be offset by any other outstanding balance owed by or to the customer. Please allow 4 to 6 weeks for delivery. Offer available while quantities last.

Your Privacy—The Harlequin® Reader Service is committed to protecting your privacy. Our Privacy Policy is available online at www.ReaderService.com or upon request from the Harlequin Reader Service.

We make a portion of our mailing list available to reputable third parties that offer products we believe may interest you. If you prefer that we not exchange your name with third parties, or if you wish to clarify or modify your communication preferences, please visit us at www.ReaderService.com/consumerschoice or write to us at Harlequin Reader Service Preference Service, P.O. Box 9062, Buffalo, NY 14269. Include your complete name and address.

HD13R

"It would be better for you if I was here full-time," Keaton said.

"How do you figure?"

"Have you considered what will happen if Grace is up all night? If I'm here we can take turns getting up with her." He could see Lark was weakening. "It makes sense."

"Let me sleep on it tonight?" She held out her hands for the baby.

"Sure."

Only, Lark never got the chance to sleep. Neither did Keaton. Shortly after Grace finished eating, she began to fuss. During the second hour of the baby's crying, Keaton searched for advice on his tablet.

"She's dry, fed and obviously tired. Why won't she sleep?"

"Because it's her first day out of the NICU and she's overstimulated."

"How about wrapping her up?" he suggested. "Says here that babies feel more secure when they're swaddled." He cued up a video and they watched it. The demonstration looked straightforward, but the woman in the video used a doll, not a real baby.

"We can try it." Lark went to the closet and returned with two blankets of different sizes. "Hopefully one of these will do the trick."

When she was done, Lark braced her hands on the dining room table and stared down at the swaddled baby. "This doesn't look right."

Keaton returned to the video. "I think we missed this part here."

Grace was growing more upset by the second and she'd managed to free her left arm.

"Is it terrible that I have no idea what I'm doing?" Lark sounded close to tears. It had been a long, stressful evening.

"Not at all. I think every first-time parent feels just as overwhelmed as we do right now."

"Thank you for sticking around and helping me."

"We're helping Grace."

The corners of her lips quivered. "Not very well, as it happens."

And then, because she looked determined and hopeless all at once, Keaton succumbed to the impulse that had been threatening to break free all week. He cupped her cheek, lowered his head and kissed her.

Don't miss BECAUSE OF THE BABY...
by Cat Schield
Available January 2015
wherever Harlequin® Desire books and ebooks are sold.

HARLEQUIN®

Desire

ALWAYS POWERFUL, PASSIONATE AND PROVOCATIVE.

SNOWED IN
WITH HER EX
by **Andrea Laurence**

Available January 2015

**Trapped in a cabin with the man who makes
her want what she shouldn't have...**

Wedding photographer Briana Harper never
expected to run into her ex at an engagement shoot!
And when a blizzard strands them...alone...in a
remote mountain cabin, she knows she's in trouble.
She's never forgotten Ian Lawson, but none of the reasons
they broke up have changed. He's still a workaholic.
And now he's an *engaged* workaholic!

But Ian is also still a man who knows what he wants.
And what he wants is Briana. Untangling the lies of his
current engagement leaves him free to...indulge.
Yet proving he's changed may be this music mogul's
toughest negotiation yet...

SNOWED IN WITH HER EX

is the first installment in **Andrea Laurence's**
Brides and Belles series:

~ Wedding planning is their business...and their pleasure ~

*Available wherever Harlequin® Desire
books and ebooks are sold.*

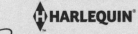